Penguin Books
ONE OF THE WATTLE BIRDS

Jessica Anderson has published six novels and a
collection of short stories, and has also written a
number of plays and adaptations for radio.
Two of her novels, *Tirra Lirra by the River* and
The Impersonators, won the Miles Franklin
Award in 1978 and 1980 respectively. *The
Impersonators* also won the New South Wales
Premier's Award in 1981. Her *Stories from the
Warm Zone* won the *Age* Book of the Year
Award and the FAW Barbara Ramsden Award in
1987.

Jessica Anderson was born in Brisbane, and
apart from a few years in Europe during her
youth, she has spent most of her life in
Sydney, where she still lives.

Other books by Jessica Anderson

An Ordinary Lunacy (1963)
The Last Man's Head (1970)
The Commandant (1975)
Tirra Lirra by the River (1978)
The Impersonators (1980)
Stories from the Warm Zone (1987)
Taking Shelter (1990)

ONE OF THE WATTLE BIRDS

Jessica Anderson

Penguin Books

Penguin Books Australia Ltd
487 Maroondah Highway, PO Box 257
Ringwood, Victoria 3134, Australia
Penguin Books Ltd
Harmondsworth, Middlesex, England
Viking Penguin, A Division of Penguin Books USA Inc.
375 Hudson Street, New York, New York 10014, USA
Penguin Books Canada Limited
10 Alcorn Avenue, Toronto, Ontario, Canada M4V 3B2
Penguin Books (N.Z.) Ltd
182-190 Wairau Road, Auckland 10, New Zealand

First published by Penguin Books Australia, 1994
10 9 8 7 6 5 4 3 2 1
Copyright © Jessica Anderson

Typeset in 12/14pt Caslon 540 by Midland Typesetters, Maryborough, Victoria
Made and printed in Australia by Australian Print Group

National Library of Australia
Cataloguing-in-Publication data:

Jessica Anderson
One of the Wattle Birds
ISBN 014 024032 2.
1. Title.
A823.3

WEDNESDAY
THE LIBRARY

WHENEVER I LOOK up, I see Wil getting on with it.

This morning, when the drilling started, he jumped up and said, 'Right. That's it. Let's go to the library, where we can get on with it.'

They are renovating a bathroom and kitchen on the second floor of our crummy old building. When they started, yesterday, Wil went up and talked to the two renovators, then came back and said with deadly calm, 'There goes the whole of stu-vac.'

So he stuffed his work in his bag and went to the library, and I stayed home and put silicone plugs in my ears, and a headset on, and read Malory.

Muffled like that, the drilling turned out to be helpful. It supplied the underlying distraction I need to help me concentrate.

This need probably formed when I used to do homework to the sound of Mum's word processor in the front room, or to the music she put on when she stopped.

Which means the kind of noise I need is mechanical and impersonal.

But in that case, why can I concentrate when Wil and I sit together at our long work table in the flat?

Possible answer: Nothing, nothing, is more impersonal than Wilfred Bonar Meade when he is concentrating on his work. He removes his presence by magic, and becomes merely a stationary source of rustles and shuffles and soft tappings.

I didn't actually want to come to the library today, either. So why did I just tag along with Wil? Possibly because I had a sort of restless feeling starting, and also because I thought, Oh well, I could do with a look at Vinaver.

So now there Wil is, over there, impaled to his work. And here I am, over here, unable to get a look at Vinaver – reserved, reserved – and pretending to be waiting for Morton, which I already know is no help, and doing this because I can't just sit here whistling, can I?

Fisher was too crowded, so we had to come in here to the State. I feel all right in here if I can get one of the little cubicles along the side, but not at these big tables out in the open. The little noises come from too many directions, and also you can't help looking up at all that glass above you. People going up to the main entrance can actually look down and see you. Just then I put my head back and met someone's eyes. I tried not to look hostile.

Jesus, Wil would say. They're tax payers. They own the place.

And I know that, I know they do. But the people walking soundlessly by up there, plus all the tiny secretive noises down here, make me restless.

I don't agree that that's neurotic.

Did I mean to bring in this airmail pad? I think so, though they are so light and thin you can easily gather them up with your notebooks.

I also have a new blue refill for my pen.

This is Cecily Ambruss's new pen. Her new blue refill makes a thin blue satisfying line.

This is one of the six airmail pads Cecily Ambruss bought in Verona a hundred years ago.

Or, to be more specific, last year, when she was there with her friends, when she and her friends were still a sextet.

Cecily and Wil
Katie and Sean
Rachel and Athol

Today, in the State Library, Sydney, Cecily and Wil sit a long way apart, because of Wil's impalement.

When Wil makes a note, he jerks his head forward, like a pigeon.

Though he is not even slightly like a pigeon. He is usually beautiful, and Cecily usually loves him.

Wilfred Bonar Meade is much better looking than Cecily Ambruss. That is an accepted fact (in fact).

Cecily Ambruss was described recently, for the purpose of identification, like this:

One of those skinny toothy girls, with real thick dry frizzy hair.

'Let us say nothing,' Mum would have said, 'about that odious use of the word real.'

'It's real common nowadays,' she might have added.

That's the second time Mum's got in here. Go away, Mum.

Wil just looked across at me. Wilfred Bonar Meade just smiled at me.

Wilfred Bonar Meade is pleased as anything because he thinks I'm getting on with it.

I feel a bit offended. He usually understands me better than that. He knows I'm not going to fail. He knows I always do well.

Law's different. It's different for Wilfred Bonar Meade. Law's more exacting than English.

When he's not impaled he understands my refusal to be got at by pre-examination fever. He agrees with it. So why, now, just at the last minute, does he have to go and catch it?

My relaxation about exams never seemed to bother Mum, not even when at the last minute I would find some terribly urgent and quite unrelated thing to do.

'No doubt you have your own way of working,' she used to say.

But not as if she cared.

She won't go away, so I'll let her in for a bit, but won't let it develop into another bout.

Not as if she cared. I interpreted that (if I bothered to interpret it at all) as policy. But was it indifference? In that and in other matters? Is indifference the answer to the question that keeps coming back, and keeps coming back?

So, the case for indifference: You get to be Mum's age, and you just develop a vast interior fund of indifference. It doesn't show much, but it's there, and in a crisis, such as your own impending death, you can draw on it. You can let it take over and obliterate anything that might disturb it, or you.

And also, it can let you look at people as if they were complete strangers, or even objects.

When I think of that look she used to give me, just before I went away, I feel coming over my own face the coolness, the quietness, the courtesy of her expression.

Or am I making that look of hers more significant than it actually was because now I am able to contribute her knowledge that she was dying? Whereas, at the time, I hadn't (as she would say) the slightest idea.

'I haven't the slight-est idea.'

I hadn't the slightest idea because, as she would also say, she did not see fit to inform me.

I can't talk to anyone about this (except Uncle Nick when available) because I talked so much about it at first that they all got sick of it, and started putting up guards if I got anywhere near the subject. Especially after I had been to Mr Parry.

Professional help makes you lose your entitlement.

At first, though, Wil would listen, and so would Rachel and Katie. Apart from Uncle Nick, Rachel and Katie were the best. We were still a sextet then, though on the verge of shattering.

When I described that look to Rachel and Katie, Rachel was really interested, and asked if Mum had been a bit catatonic, or slightly epileptic, and was having what they called 'absences'. But I said no (though I checked later with Gran), and then Rachel and Katie speculated about drugs she might have been prescribed, but I shook my head again, because I had asked her doctor about that. And then Katie lost patience, and mentioned Mr Parry, and also said that it must have advantages to be able to see people as strangers, or even objects, and that she wished she could see Sean like that.

'All too familiar, I'm starting to think,' said Katie.

And just after that, Katie left Sean, waving her arms about and refusing to discuss it, and dropped out, and went to Amsterdam. Amsterdam!

Katie and I had been best friends since we were both eight, and that was the first time she had done anything important without telling me first.

There was only a card from Bangkok, saying she would write, which she hasn't.

And just after Katie went off into the blue, Rachel and Athol changed direction and enrolled in an agricultural course at North Ryde. They are both very physical people, and Rachel's parents are farmers, so it makes sense, but it means we hardly ever see them.

And just after *that*, Sean turned up with a Chinese girlfriend. Or, I should say, Cantonese. Her name is Chun-Ling, and she is very beautiful, incredibly slight and fragile and delicately made. But Wil and I couldn't help being disconcerted by the way she kept giggling. Most of the Chinese we know were quiet to start with, and we didn't mind that she never instigated any conversation, but when you know that if you address a person directly she will burst out giggling, invariably, it's inhibiting. We know that what Sean says is true, and that it's only a nervous habit, and after the exams we are going to try again, and take a more sensitive approach.

Wil and I don't need to put up the quote signs when there are only the two of us. A more sensitive approach, we say. No signals, no irony.

Though it's up to Sean too. He will have to stop telling us to piss off.

We miss those four. We haven't made new friends because of Wil's impalement. And, it has to be said, because of my bouts.

I miss them more than Wil does, especially Katie. Katie and I watched the same TV, saw the same films, and read the same books. Together we decided to limit the dash and the exclamation mark, and to favour the bracket and the elegant colon. And together, or with my cousin Eugene, we went dancing, usually to gay dance parties where heteros could dance without being sexually checked out all the time. After you got warmed up, there was just the dancing. Dancing, I would see Katie, I would see Eugene, miles away, dancing. That was happiness, that dancing, to music that lifted you, and poised you, and melted your bones.

Then, after Katie and I had each had a few sexual disasters, and were in a state of real but hilarious despair, we both fell in love in the same week, not with the types we had fancied before, but with Wil and Sean, who had to be classed as Serious Guys.

We didn't see each other much after that, and didn't care much either, until the sextet drifted together, and made the plan to go back-packing through Europe and India together, and actually *did* it, in spite of all the dramas and difficulties and hold-ups, and in the doing of it we formed, or fused. At least, that's what I thought we had done. And Katie was a vital part of that fusion. At least, that's what I thought she was.

Wil says, 'Yes, sure I miss them, but that's the way it goes.' And I know that. I know that's the way it goes. But that doesn't stop me from waking up sometimes and thinking, Where are they? And then, no matter what I do, up creeps this thing about Mum. And I get this ache, or worse, this feeling of wild incredulity. And then the babble of protest starts up. And the anger. Not much, not like it was, but as if I'm engaged in a permanent low-key quarrel, and don't even know who my antagonist is.

Quite often, I pick on Katie. I open our letter box and bang it shut. 'It wouldn't hurt her to *write*.'

Wil laughs. 'When was Katie reliable?'

I rang Katie's mother. 'Oh yes,' said Katie's mother. And she laughed. 'Oh yes, certainly she keeps in touch. She rings when she needs money.'

Katie used to say that her parents were genuinely

cynical, and that it wasn't just a pose. She used to sound rather boastful about it.

'She promised to write to you?' said Katie's mother. 'Promised? Katie?' And she laughed again.

I often wish Eugene was still in Sydney, and we could go dancing together, though I know in my heart it wouldn't work.

Wil says I miss the others more than he does because I wasn't brought up in a family, but alone with Mum. He also says that I idealise the sextet and our journey together. But I don't think so. I don't think I do. I haven't forgotten the quarrels, or the tension when we were trying to avoid a quarrel, and for all I know, the others might have had horrible times, like I did at Lucca, because of course we didn't stay together all the time, but some days broke away into singles or pairs, and came back together at night. But we had a kind of harmony that was able to absorb the sticks and stones, and it wasn't until we got home, and I was still getting over hearing about Mum, that it dawned on me that maybe harmony like that happens only once in your life.

It isn't as if we had to work at it all the time, either. We seemed to have a sort of immunity. For example, we drank a lot some nights, but it didn't make us mean and critical, like it started to do soon after we got back.

Mum would say, 'Like? Do you mean As?'

As it started to do soon after we got back.

One night, fairly soon after we got back, when we had been drinking, Katie said (This was in the

Min'h Hai, just before she broke with Sean) Katie said that in the eighteen months she had known Sean, he had never said one essentially serious word to her. She repeated that she was speaking of essences, of fundamentals. And, Oh yes, she said, she remembered all our great conversations over there, but to her alone, away from the group, he never said one serious word except when they quarrelled, and that was because expletives were governed by a different part of the brain than other speech.

We all laughed, and Katie laughed too, but kept saying she meant it. Sean said that when Katie said Serious, she meant Exciting, and that Katie was a Sensationalist. I thought I was the only one who heard this, because we were all still laughing, and Katie was still pointing around the table and saying in her carrying voice that she absolutely meant it.

Then Rachel said, looking at Athol in that tender way she has, that Athol wasn't as bad as that, but did have that tendency, and that perhaps it was a fault endemic in the Australian male character.

Athol and Wil groaned and said, Oh, not that again. Fair go. It used to be, sure. Inherited British militarism, and so on. But not now. Sean didn't say anything, but just hunched up. And then Rachel and I joined Katie, not really meaning it, but because we were a bit drunk, and for solidarity and so on, we three joined together and chanted, Aussie feller never change, Aussie feller just the same.

Wil laughed and said, Hey, hey, steady on. And he took hold of my wrist and flapped my hand about. And then Sean said loudly that in his opinion, you could talk too bloody much.

'You can wheedle away too much at trifling emotional detail,' said Sean. And then he blurted out, 'You can kill the bird in the egg.'

A certain amount of hell then broke loose. Katie jumped to her feet and said in a light, clear, almost singing voice, 'So the bird is supposed to spend its whole life in the egg.'

And then it was all chaos and babble and shouting and laughing until Sean abruptly got up and went out. Then it was silent. Then Wil, who was still holding my wrist, said quietly, 'Don't you love Cec's little Egyptian wrists?' And we began to talk of hands, and fingers, and harpists, and guitarists, but were tired, and the night was over.

But on the way home, Wil stopped us both under a tristania tree and said he had better tell me he agreed with Sean about Katie. 'Katie is a sensationalist. That's spot-on.'

'Then if you heard Sean say that, back there,' I said, indignantly pointing, 'why didn't you agree with him, back there?'

'It's not worth opposing Katie. All you get in return are wild suppositions and inflated feelings.'

'Katie's a romantic. What's wrong with that?'

'Nothing. Provided you're able to reconcile it with truth and proportion.'

'Truth,' I said. 'Here you are, standing under a tree, thinking you know what truth is, yet you accuse Katie of inflation.'

Wil laughed, and put an arm across my shoulders,

and walked us on. When Wil puts an arm across my shoulders, I can't help feeling comforted, and even safe. I know it's only an illusion, but I can't help it.

But under the next tristania tree, he stopped us again. 'All the same, Cec, you had better tell me if you really think I'm incapable, with you, of serious conversation.'

And I said no, of course I didn't. I had a hopeless feeling starting, and not to give in to it, I said, 'But sometimes when I feel I must talk about something –' and he broke in and said, 'It's true I don't like it when you can't stop talking about your mother.'

'It isn't only that,' I said. The hopelessness was like a balloon, opening out of my body. It was a relief, really.

'I think you can talk to feed an obsession,' said Wil.

'There are other things,' I said, 'apart from that.'

'Associated things,' he said.

'I don't know,' I said, not just being evasive and sulky, but because sometimes I think everything in the world is associated with my mother's death. So I said, 'Things I can't say to anyone else at all,' and I don't add, Now that she's dead, and Katie's gone, because I don't want to start crying again. Something was pending for Wil then, too. Not an exam, but some busy-ness, blocking up paths.

'Well,' said Wil, 'if you try not to be obsessive, I'll try leaving myself more open. Right?'

He said this in true, reasonable, Mr Parry style. So in a sort of reflex action I said, Right. Not meaning it particularly, but just sick of the whole thing.

Yet the episode did turn out to be of help,

because after that night in the Min'h Hai, if I mentioned Mum, Wil would put on his attentive face. It
was a bit too attentive, that face, but it was better than
before. And in return, I would keep my talk about
Mum hovering about the level of my real perplexity.
Usually, I would circle my perplexity by talking
about the money, and by asking him if he believed he
and I would still be together if Mum hadn't put it in
her will that I am to inherit the money from the
sale of her half of the house only when I marry. And
Wil doesn't laugh now, and say, Of course not, and
that everybody knows he's in it only for the sake of
my vast fortune. And he doesn't get angry, either,
and walk off saying, What shit. No, now, though he
sometimes says that the limit of his marital ambition is to live in a flat with its own laundry (Wil
hates the laundromat) he is more likely to point out
that we didn't even know about the money (not the
bloody money any more) until we came back from our
journey, and then to go on to say that in his opinion,
he and I stay together for the same reason we got
together, which is because we love one another.

Love one another. Those words can still stun my
perplexity.

I just looked across at Wil and saw that he was
looking at me, not as if he saw me, but remotely, as if
his brain had no energy to spare for its visual function.
Then he sort of woke up, and smiled, and I smiled
back, and then we both put our heads down.

Once, when he and I were talking about the
money, he did say, seriously, that it had occurred to
him that if we ever wanted children, the money

would be a consideration. Not as important as the laundry, he couldn't help saying, but all the same, a consideration, and that a marriage ceremony would be simpler, and a lot cheaper, than a legal challenge to that clause. And that, he said, must have occurred to me too.

I agreed that it had, and might have done even if Aunt Gail hadn't mentioned it six or seven or maybe thirty-five times. But when I wouldn't go past saying that it had occurred to me, he said, Okay, let it rest.

So that I didn't have to go on to say that I have no wish at all to have children, and that frankly, I see so little point in maternity that I can't imagine why anyone wants children. I let that rest, too. At first I used to tell Wil everything, but slowly a sort of suspended list has developed, of things I will tell him one day.

From memory, Wil asked that question about children just after the sale of the house. I had always thought of the house as Mum's (Our House) but it turned out to be owned jointly by her and Uncle Nick. It was left to them, half each, by their father, my grandfather Lorenzo Ambruss. Though I ought to say Ambrussi, because Uncle Nick told me that in his will he had picked up the i, and signed it Lorenzo Ambrussi.

My grandfather Lorenzo Ambrussi was an almost unknown figure to me. Sometimes I get a blurred image of a red waistcoat, but mostly I remember him because of the family assembly after his funeral, to which Eugene and I went when we were both six, and which was the first and only time I have seen his younger son, my Uncle Ugo.

Everybody loves Ugo.

Gran's satisfied way of saying that turned it into a family saying. After Granddad died, whenever Gran paid us a visit, Mum used to go round singing it.

'Every-body l'hoves Ugo.'

Which, I see now, gave it an edge of irony. Even though everybody *did* love Ugo. Especially Gran, of course, but Mum too. Ugo was eight years younger than Mum, so she could remember him as a fat little adorable baby. I can remember him as a fat little neat man, and I remember his husky caressing voice, and the honour of his close attentiveness. Eugene stood beside me, on that one and only occasion, and we both gazed upwards in fascination.

But that was all, because the next day, Uncle Ugo had to fly off to play in an orchestra in Belgrade. And after that, whenever Gran visited us in her new widowhood, she would follow Mum around talking about Ugo's asthma, and saying that someone ought to be with him, to give him a home to come home to.

And in about a year, Gran did go to be with him, settling in London so that he would have a home to come home to.

'A h'home to come h'home to,' sang Mum.

Uncle Ugo didn't share in the house, but got something else, shares I think, which Gran sold for him before she went off to make him a home to come home to. Granddad Ambrussi was fairly rich. He

made most of his money in wholesale fruit and veg-
etables, which is why Gran always says, 'I hope
you're eating up your fruit and veg. Fruit and veg
have been good to us.'

There was always a feeling hovering about that
Mum was in disgrace with Granddad, but at least,
when he left her the half-share of the house, he
didn't make any ridiculous conditions, like she did
when she put in her will that thing about marriage.

'Imagine her doing that,' I said to Uncle Nick.
'Her, of all people.'

And he said, with his patience, 'Well, we don't
have to imagine it, do we, Cec? Because here it is,
Cec, in writing. And until you marry, the money
will be safe. Though I could wish she hadn't specified
a bank.'

'And you'll HAVE THE INTEREST,' said Aunt
Gail.

'Such as it is,' said Uncle Nick. 'I could have
trebled that.'

'Yes,' I said, 'but the point is, why did she do it?
Because, listen, say nobody wants to marry me?'

'Remember she HAD MET WIL,' said Aunt
Gail. But Uncle Nick said, sober, 'I don't know how it
would stand up to a legal challenge.'

'As if I could challenge it,' I shouted.

'I don't see why not,' said Uncle Nick.

And because I couldn't explain why not, I just let
my instinctive recoil be absorbed into my general
offendedness. This was soon after I came back, and
when I wasn't crying, I was feeling angry and somehow trapped. So I raved on about the money not

being the point, and then wafted away from the point myself by saying, 'Anyone would think it made me a big heiress or something.'

But Uncle Nick said, rather pained, that the double block of land made it an attractive property, and that if he managed the sale well, which he flattered himself he would do, it would be a nice little sum.

'Enough to give a YOUNG COUPLE A GOOD START,' said Aunt Gail.

But I asked why they kept on about nice little sums and young couples when oh, all that was beside the point, when oh, it was as clear as anything that by putting that in, she was saying she regretted it. 'There,' I said, 'that's the point.'

I didn't mean that she regretted having me, exactly, but that she regretted becoming one of the first frankly single mothers, which people were not very relaxed about nineteen years ago. But Aunt Gail misunderstood me, and leaned forward and said, 'Cecily dear, NOBODY EVER REGRETS having a baby. EVER.'

And before I can get closer to what I mean, she looks right into my eyes and says, from about five centimetres away, 'You are speaking of a BIOLOGICAL IMPOSSIBILITY.'

Uncle Nick took my hands. He has lovely satisfactory warm hands, like Mum's, and I started to cry and howl all over the place. And I know now that I was repressing my real question, which was: Why did she let me go away without telling me, etcetera, and which even as early as that they had made me ashamed to keep asking.

And while I am wetting Uncle Nick's pink and white striped pure cotton shirt, and he is murmuring the name of Mr Parry, Aunt Gail leans forward and says in the fast confidential voice Mum used to call her second speech mode, 'Of course, Cec, we wrote to your father.'

'He hasn't answered yet,' says Uncle Nick. 'But it's early days yet. Early days.'

It was early days for that man for another six weeks or so, and then he wrote me a letter saying Sad News, very sorry and so on, and then saying that though he was a very busy man, he would be happy to see me if a meeting was *vital* to me (He actually did that, he underlined vital) but that he hoped I understood that his friendship with my mother was a long time ago, and that he had since assumed many obligations etc. and etc. So I wrote back saying Thank you for your letter, and I couldn't really see any point in a meeting, and tra-la-la and so on.

After that, if Wil mentioned my father, which he was inclined to do, I would say, 'Oh, you mean that man who campaigned for population control and had eight children himself. Or maybe nine.' And that I didn't know if I was included in the count or not. And nor did I care. And that that was enough of him.

And though still, sometimes, I drop into a fairly sultry rumination about my father, I more often ruminate about my reluctance to challenge that marriage clause. But most often of all, I wonder why my mother let me go away without telling me she was dying, and let me stay away till it was over.

It's a relief even to write it, right out like that, since I'm not allowed to say it any more.

I don't believe it is exaggeration, or sensationalism, to say that that question harasses me. I feel like one of those raggedy birds you see trying to feed their remorseless young. And among the gaping beaks, that one gapes widest. And among the chorus of cheeps, that one cheeps loudest.

I've been given answers. By Gran on long-distance phone calls, by Mum's friends Carmen and Sandra, by Aunt Gail (of course) and by Uncle Nick (the best). Not to mention Mr Parry. And after I've carried these answers back, and dropped them in, the birds will be quiet, but then, in no time at all, the cheeping starts again.

And I couldn't help noticing that all these answers, even Uncle Nick's, gradually moulded themselves to agree with Mr Parry.

The mother bird must hate those gaping beaks sometimes. Not to be a sensationalist, I won't claim to be under the same natural compulsion as that mother bird, only that sometimes it feels like it.

Uncle Nick is even more busy than usual because of this re-location Aunt Gail keeps telling me about (to ward me off). Uncle Nick is as bad as Wil for busy-ness.

I hate it in here. Not only because of the wrong noises and the glassy spaces, but because it smells of plastic.

Also, I am hungry. I keep thinking of anchovies.

I just looked across at Wil in a very concentrated

way. I kept looking, and concentrating, and after about thirty seconds, he began stacking his books.

Yes, I know it is only coincidence.

However (as Mum would say), I know that when I look up again, he will have finished his stack, and will be looking across at me.

He will catch my eye, smile, nod towards the door.

And I will nod back Yes.

THURSDAY

THIS MORNING THERE
was only some light tapping, so Wil went up to see
the two renovators, whose names turn out to be
Scotty and Clark, and asked if there would be any
drilling. Certainly would be, they said, and Sorry.

So Wil came down and packed his bag, but I said
we should consider the long term, and learn to cope
with noise by changing our mental attitudes and by
using muffling devices. Wil said, Right, he would
start doing that straight after the exams. Then he
departed for the library, and I went on with Malory.

I thought I knew Malory fairly well, but last
week I realised I've neglected King Arthur himself,
and am now trying to detect by what means, as the
Tales proceed, Malory makes him more and more
modern, which means of course more like a ruler in
Malory's own time and place, which is fifteenth-
century Britain. And the example I like, and am

trying to trace, is that after the first section, Arthur is the only central figure whose fate is not changed by the intervention of magic.

That first section is crammed full of magic, and in fact is almost a contest between magicians: Merlin and the Lady of the Lake who help Arthur, and Morgan le Fay who wants to destroy him. But in the second section, all that stops, (I hope). In fact, it is announced in the title that Arthur is Emperor BY DIGNITY OF HIS OWN HANDS, which sounds promising. All the same, though I know Merlin is out of the action, imprisoned under that stone, The Lady of the Lake and Morgan le Fay are still at large, and either can work her magic in one line, even in five words, so I am forcing myself to scrutinise all but the first of the Tales again.

The tapping got louder, but with my muffling devices on, though it was not the ideal impersonal distraction, it didn't disturb me much. Yet something disturbed me. Something kept coming between my mind and the page. It was like when you come out of sunlight into a darkish room, and coloured squiggles of light flow swiftly before your eyes and away, and you can't trace the path of one because there's always another racing after it. It was just like that. Until all of a sudden I took off the headset, and took out one plug, and went and stood by the bed, and rang Uncle Nick's office.

I hoped he would have time for coffee, if not lunch. I imagined him saying, 'Cecily dear, why not?' But then his secretary came on, and said he wasn't in today, but was working at home.

I felt my hope seeping away. But I rang the house, and one of the twins answered. I asked if that was Hilary or Brett, and she said, in her soft little voice, 'Brett.'

Mum used to say, when I came home from visiting at Uncle Nick's, 'And did you see those two with the non-gender-specific names and the eyes?' And I would hunch my shoulders forward and say in mock terror, 'The eyes certainly saw me.'

I ask for Uncle Nick, and Brett says, 'Here's Mummy.'

'Hello darling,' says Aunt Gail, as vivacious as anything. 'HOW ARE YOU? And how is THAT DELECTABLE WIL?'

I say he's impaled, and then I say yes, that's exactly what I mean, he's impaled to his work, and I agree that I should be too, and that exams are important, and then I ask why the twins are home from school, and she says because she has to take them to the dentist, and then I feel free to ask if I may speak to Uncle Nick.

'Darling he's IMPALED TOO. In his office with ALL HIS TECHNOLOGY. And a client I think.'

I hear Brett or Hilary say, Ooo he is not, and Aunt Gail says lightly and quickly, running all her words together in second speech mode, 'Yes a client so sorry Cec. Let's make another time.'

And before I can answer, she says enthusiastically, 'Let's MAKE A TIME NOW.'

I stare at the ear plug, which I am rolling into a ball, and say that exams start on Monday, and that I must work on the weekend.

'Oh CEC YOU MUST. And in any case THE WEEKEND –'

'Half an hour,' I say, quick and desperate, 'Saturday morning.'

'Oh Cec,' she says, full of grief, 'that's SUCH A BAD TIME.'

'Look,' I say, 'I have a specific question. Half an hour.'

'A BAD TIME,' she says, still full of grief but reproachful too. Then she says, very fast, 'About Chris, isn't it?'

'Yes,' I say. I hold up the silicone sphere between a thumb and forefinger, as if it's important to judge its exact shape. 'Yes,' I say, 'it's about my mother.'

'Oh darling,' she says, rather absently, 'Nick and I think of you all the time. It's only that with this re-location we're TRYING TO DO, he's so very VERY BUSY.'

I say nothing. I stare at my silicone sphere and feel helpless. I don't know why Aunt Gail gives me this hypnotised feeling. Maybe because I admired her so much when I was little, like the twins do now.

Suddenly she says, 'And darling girl, EXAMS ARE IMPORTANT.'

'I know,' I say, dull as mud. I stare at my sphere. I don't care any more. I would ring off if I weren't hypnotised.

'All the same,' she says, 'COME and talk to Nick on Saturday. YOU DO THAT, Cec.'

I'm confused. Also suspicious. I stare at the sphere and ask if she's sure he'll be home. He's an accountant and business consultant, and he really is busy. That part's true, about the busy-ness.

But Aunt Gail is shouting happily, 'Oh but IF IT'S VERY EARLY. Say, nine?'

'Right,' I say. 'Nine.'

'Only,' she adds in second-speech mode, 'I had better check with you really early. Say seven-thirty. Is that too early to ring on a Saturday?'

I don't say anything. Sometimes, when Mum was talking to Aunt Gail on the phone, she would cover the mouthpiece and say to me, 'I love it when Gail starts opening her options,' and I would look at her chillingly and say afterwards, 'You're so meee-an about Auntie Gail.'

'Shall I do that, Cec darling?' Aunt Gail is saying with a kind of intimate enthusiasm. 'Oh and BY THE WAY, Cec, I've got something exciting to tell you. It's ABOUT ME, for a change.'

I want to sigh. But I don't. I don't even do that. I concentrate on squashing the plug into a medallion on the bedside table.

'Cec, IS ANYTHING WRONG?'

'Nothing new,' I say.

'Then we'll do that, shall we?'

'All right,' I say.

And she says, as if it's a delicious secret, 'THAT'S BEST.'

And before I know it, we've finished speaking, and I'm sitting there dopily trying to pick the silicone off the table. Then I get up and float over to my half of our work table and find my place in Malory, and the corresponding place in my notes. I actually do that. Then I ask myself dully why I didn't say, It's about my money instead of *It's about my mother.* I am holding my head in my hands and staring down at the page and feeling really stupefied. But then suddenly I'm on my feet and jumping up and down and shouting at the top of my voice, What am I? A worm or something? Not that anyone could have heard, because that's when the drilling began, without warning, the noise simply exploding into the room.

I started crying with rage, then I shouted SHUT UP, and grabbed Malory, and put him in my bag, and went out still sniffing, running down the steps, not even leaving a note for Wil in case he gets home first, and not even raising and slamming the lid of the letter box.

The traffic in Parramatta Road was nearly as bad as the drilling, though less personal-sounding. I get a 436 bus so packed that a man with one of those sideways-spreading paunches was pressing it into my ribs. In the Roman buses, men used to feel us up. It was unbelievable. We thought at first it must be accidental, but we soon learned to say, in really spiteful ferocious Italian, Leave me alone. The Italian language is good for spite and ferocity, and we had a fine competitive time rehearsing it at night.

But nobody on the 436 was feeling anybody up. All the racial strands were sitting and standing and staring and dreaming on the 436, and the man with the jellyfish paunch was clearing his throat.

At the cinema complex there is an exodus, old people stepping down stiff and sideways at the front, and us at the side dropping down loose and any-old-how.

As I cross Bathurst Street I hear Wil laughing and telling me to stop walking as if the ground is hot. He would be putting a hand on the back of my neck as he said that. I slow down. I also stop craning my neck, which the twins would notice at once if I'm unlucky enough to arrive before Aunt Gail takes them to the dentist.

It's a perfect windless early summer day. To delay going underground, I walk to the far entrance of the station. In the shadows of the plane trees in Town Hall Square hundreds of pigeons are strutting about and coo-ing in their loud vengeful way. I thud down the steps thinking I ought to have cleaned my shoes, and while waiting on the platform I get out my hairbrush and give a few hopeless tugs at my hair.

But I am wearing the beautiful shirt I bought in Calcutta. The colours are so vivid yet so soft, the pattern so free yet so formal. And it is dignified to put this true art onto cheap open-weave cotton.

I get into one of the silver trains. I sit on the right hand side at first because on days like this I love the startlement of that first sight of the harbour stretching away and glittering all silent and silver and blue right out to the Heads. To stop myself from going into a fantasy about living in a beautiful house right on the edge of it, I remind myself of certain remarks of Mum's about my covetousness, and then of Gran, (who did actually live on the edge of it once) saying that her favourite Impossible Moment would be to enter Sydney Harbour on a thirties passenger liner in November 1787.

But when I asked, Why November? she said, Ah, the jacarandas.

That was last year, when I went to see her in London. It was hot in London. She wore a sleeveless dress, and I tried not to see the bagginess of the upper arm extended along the back of her pink velvet sofa. She's eighty-something.

The only Impossible Moment I'm interested in at present would be sitting opposite Mum at the kitchen table and saying, 'Well, come on, why did you let me go away etc, etc? And incidentally and by the way, why did you look at me as if I were a new species, or an object?'

Then I wouldn't be in this train, going up to harass poor Uncle Nick.

After we cross the bridge, I change over to the left hand side, out of the sun, and open Malory. The carriage is nearly empty. The only time these trains are crowded is in peak hours and school holidays. When I was little, and Mum used to take me to the city, she used to say that she supposed the wretched trains would be packed with gnomes and beasts. And of course, my generational loyalty made me protest on behalf of the gnomes, and later, of the beasts. And though at my own bestial stage I often went in alone or with Katie and other beasts, I was still very brittle about that label, and was the more offended because she would only laugh.

She seemed different from other mothers not only because she was single (which Katie had made me quite proud of), but because she was older. She had me when she was thirty-eight, which was unusual at a time when, to use her words again, nobody was deafened by the chorus of biological clocks ticking.

Now that I have forty minutes alone, and the noise of the train as the perfect underlying distraction, I get out Malory and go on with my scanning. It is unlikely that either the Lady of the Lake or Morgan le Fay will appear to help or hinder Arthur now that he has crossed the Channel with his knights and is on his way to conquer the Romans, but improbability hasn't stopped them before, so I can't skip at all. He slays a giant without magic intervention, and I pass cautiously through rich Lombardy and Tuskayne, and to Rome and the battle where the usual blood and brains are sticking to their swords, and so far, everything has been done by dignity of his own hands, and I am almost at the end of the tale when my attention starts hopping and skipping, and I realise this is because we are about to come into Turramurra.

I sit up straight and slew my eyes sideways. I am not going to funk this again. But the windows are smaller than in the old red trains, so I quickly shove Malory into my bag, get up, and go and stand in the doorway. I put my bag at my feet, fold my arms, and observe, through the glass of the door, the clipped trees on the neat platform, and the rose bushes on the grassy slope between the train lines and the trees up top. And I see Mum putting out a hand as she walked to the door of the train when I was still little and had to be met. I see the easy movement of her tall figure, her arm always fully outstretched, her dark clothes, her cropped grey and ginger hair, and always that outstretched arm. Then I have to remind myself that she wasn't always alone. Now and again she would be with another mother, or with one of the old travelling companions who had turned up, and sometimes I would be with other kids. But it has remained a dominant image because we would both be alone nine times out of ten, because, for one thing, I would push in front of the other kids so that I could tumble out and start telling her things, and for another, the old companions hardly ever came, and the other mothers waited up on the east side in their cars, and we lived on the west, and had no car. I would start telling her things as I tumbled out of the train and would keep on as I laboured up those long steps, leaning forward and splaying my feet in their great big laced-up shoes, and banging the step in front of me with the end of my school case, which I wouldn't let her carry because it was MINE.

If we went into Severs' shop on the way home, and she talked to Mrs Severs, I would dig her in the leg and tell her in a loud whisper to hurry up, and then she would take my hand and squeeze and stroke it as they finished their conversation, talking about gardening and cooking and Jascha Heifetz, shutting their eyes and saying that records are only a reminder, and that they don't compare, simply don't compare, while she stroked my hand or the back of my neck. Her forbearance annoyed me because it felt less like kindness or absent-mindedness than a kind of self-containment I wanted to broach. Yet her smile as she comes to the door of the train, with her arm extended, I can never see as anything less than joyful. I have tried, but there it always is, that joy and delight.

She must have been forty-something then, so it's possible the joy and delight wore off rather quickly. I remember the time she offered me twenty cents to stop talking for ten minutes. I can't remember whether I took it or not.

When the train moves again, I pick up my bag and lean sideways against the wall, with my eyes shut, recapitulating my reading of Malory so far, until the train comes into my stop. Then I jump out and bound up the long stairs as if I had an urgent appointment, and suddenly I feel the fresh air meet my skin. It's so warm and fresh and surprising that I stand still and shut my eyes, as if that's the only way the pores of my skin can drink it in.

You forget, you actually forget, how rotten and fumy the air is down there.

As I stand there, suddenly, out of the blue, I see Mum at the train when her face showed no joy and surprise. There I am, waiting to tumble out and tell her things, and there she is, standing with one of the old companions, Gerard Someone, and both of them laughing almost uncontrollably. Mum is actually wiping away tears of laughter, and doesn't see me, or I think she doesn't, so I make myself stumble and almost fall, and when she hurries forward, stretching out that arm, her face is serious, and she is saying something like, Oh Cec, I'm sorry.

Gerard Scott or Scutt turned up more often than

the others. Katie (of course) said he was her lover, but I never saw any evidence of it.

There is a short cut to Uncle Nick's, but to give Aunt Gail and the twins more time to leave the house, I go the long way. The jacarandas and flame trees are in flower, and here and there mauve and red petals make intersecting pools on the footpath. The ashes and maples and so on are all in their absolutely unblemished early summer leaf, and high up you can hear that whispering of the tall eucalypts and see how the leaves flicker from green to silver, silver to green, always.

And of course there are birds. Hundreds of birds. Magpies and currawongs are carolling high up, and as I pass a grevillea bush a flock of tiny fat birds like musical notes dash inside it and twitter around in there and then dash urgently out and swing away and curve upwards into the sky.

And naturally, that sky is blue. It is what we used to call, to mock our own homesickness in Europe, a true-tourist-blue.

Now and again I hear the Doik bird make his single statement. DOIK. But he is overwhelmed by the rest. I think you have to be alone in a house for days on end before the Doik bird can get to you.

Katie also intrudes, but I shut her out. I walk slowly. A cat sits on a wall ignoring me with wide-open eyes. A red setter lopes up to a fence and looks at me anxiously. One car passes. On the opposite pavement, a woman carrying an airline bag walks quickly to the station. A cleaner, not Aunt Gail's. I take deep luxurious breaths and struggle with a covetous fantasy of Wil and me living up here with a dog and a cat in a modest hut in a huge garden which is also within walking distance of the Min'h Hai and the Red Rose, and quite near a good beach.

But I am able to laugh.

Goodbye doggie. Goodbye pussy.

I'm getting better at reminding myself that daydreaming is enfeebling. To say nothing, as Mum would say, of covetous.

Now I let Katie in too. She is tossing her hair over one shoulder and talking about the constipated middle classes.

Though I was never as manic as Katie about the middle classes. 'You'll have to come to terms with them,' Mum would say to Katie and me, in our kitchen. And when Katie would swing her hair about and say Never, Never, Mum would say, 'Well, you don't have to make it the mission of your life.'

Katie didn't include Mum and me in the middle classes because of my illegitimacy, as it was still called there and then. That was my initial attraction for Katie. 'Cec's mother is single,' she would say to other girls, not exactly boasting. Until, inevitably, one replied, 'So is mine.' And later, of younger girls, 'And hers. And hers.' But by the time I lost that distinction, we had become real friends. She forgave my attacks of common sense, and I forgave her chronic unpunctuality, forgetting my anger, when she finally did turn up, because her running step, her secretive grin, her glee, always made it seem as if she had something exciting to impart. Which she sometimes did.

Uncle Nick's house stands at the bottom of a sloping garden, so you hardly see it from the street. I walk very slowly down the shallow stone steps under the jasmine arch where Eugene and I used to wrestle and whisper and groan and try to eat each other. I suppose you could say that Eugene was my first lover. He was having serious strife in that house down there, and after a last big bust-up he left home and went to Melbourne, where after various crises he managed to get into Melbourne Uni. He's on Austudy and is fairly broke, but every couple of weeks or so he has a few drinks and rings me and says, 'It is still you, Cec, it is only you.'

I'm sure that is not as lugubrious as it sounds.

As I cross the lawn my confidence that Aunt Gail will have left melts away. I feel intimidated but stubborn, and make my usual vow not to let her hypnotise me this time. I can't do anything about the nervous blush rising to my face. I notice that the front door and all the windows are now pro- tected by security grilles. I am not going to the front door, but over to the kitchen-breakfast-family room on the eastern side.

Here the security door stands open and hooked back, and through the bronze wire mesh I see Aunt Gail standing at the long table, arranging things on a tray, and the twins lounging and weaving about. I renew my vow, touch the bell as I push open the door, and step inside.

Aunt Gail looks up.

When Mum and Aunt Gail were in the feminist movement together, Aunt Gail was in great demand as a speaker. 'I swear,' said Mum, 'she was like that spell-binder in *The Bostonians*. Verena. Especially in small groups. It was partly the eyes.'

Aunt Gail does have extraordinary eyes. It isn't only that they're huge, and true blue, and so on, it's their swiftness and expressiveness. Now, instantly, they fill with her piteous reproachful look. This makes the blue look wet, yet it isn't really suffused. It's mysterious, how she does that. The wet piteous look lasts two seconds, then she's looking at the tray again and muttering absent-mindedly, 'Oh it's you, Cec. Now what's missing from this tray. Oh, I know. The strainer. Hilary, get me the strainer.'

When Hilary does that, Aunt Gail gives me the eyes again, dry and snappy this time, and says, 'This is a LOVELY SURPRISE, Cec. I'm just taking this tray to YOUR UNCLE AND HIS CLIENT.'

'I hoped the client would have gone by now,' I say.

'He's just arrived,' says Brett.

'Put some SUGAR in that little POT, Brett.'

'Nobody takes sugar these days,' says Brett.

'BRETT!'

'He's Daddy's first client today,' says Brett, as she does this.

He's the client I told Cecily DADDY WAS EXPECTING,' says Aunt Gail comfortably. She picks up the tray and as she passes me tilts her face and says, 'Kiss-kiss.'

I kiss her cheek. For a woman of forty-something she has marvellous skin. After she goes, Hilary and Brett prance forward holding their arms wide and saying, 'Kiss-kiss.'

I kiss each of them on her exquisite forehead. Then I sit down, put my bag on the table, fold my arms beside it, and say, 'I thought you two were going to the dentist.'

'Not till two o'clock,' says Brett.

'So you took the morning off too?'

'It's only yucky gym this morning,' Brett tells me. She folds her arms opposite mine on the table, supporting herself while the rest of her dances and jigs about. Hilary does that for a while, too, then sidles up beside me, looks at my shirt, and says, 'You got that in India.'

'Some of their things are quite nice,' says Brett politely.

'I love your bangles,' I say.

Each has a very thin silver and gold bangle on her flawless left arm. Those two left arms appear inches from my eyes, as two hands lovingly slide the bangles higher up, watched by two pairs of golden-brown eyes.

'Gran gave them to us.'

'Which Gran?'

'Gran Ambruss.'

'She sent us an ancient gold bangle, Cec. It was hers as a child. All hollow and dented. And she said, One of you have this.'

'And we rang and said, That's not fair. Which one?'

'And after a while she said, Cec, she said, All right then, throw the cat a goldfish. Go and choose two bangles the same, and I'll send the money, and that can be my advance Christmas present.'

'So we did. Twenty-two carat.'

'And that's platinum, Cec. See?'

Gran in London had rolled her eyes with amusement and terror as she spoke of the twins. I say, 'Well, lucky things, aren't you?'

The twins giggle. They once told me that when they grew up they were going to open a jewellery shop, with the window all black, and just three beautiful pieces in it, softly spotlit. But they were only six then. They're more subtle than that now. They used to look at the brand names of your jeans and shirts then too. They don't need to now. Nor do they stare. Now they take in everything at high speed, with what Gran calls the once-over. The once-over is very fast, and would look casual if you didn't notice their eyes. They are wearing blue jeans, white T-shirts of the finest (naturally) cotton, and tan plaited shoes of the kind I bought in Italy to visit my relations in Lucca. Their thick straight fair hair is perfectly sculptured, and their darker eyebrows are just naturally perfect. I wonder if they still smooth them with a spit-dampened forefinger, but suspect they use a tiny brush dipped in something or other imported.

Hilary stands uncomfortably close to me, her forearms on the table taking the weight of her jigging feet. And now she reaches out, quite deliberately, and takes the cuff of my Indian shirt between a thumb and forefinger, and gives it a squeeze just where the stitching has bunched up a bit. She actually does that. And catches Brett's eye. Brett leans on her forearms and dances happily, and I say, 'Does Eugene still call you two the fashion wankers?'

They burst out laughing and clap their hands over their mouths. The thing I like best about them is their teeth. They haven't had them straightened yet, and they're a bit buck, like mine. Brett suddenly puts her arms round my neck, and I give her a hug. Then we all hug each other, and Hilary says, 'It was style wankers, not fashion wankers.' And Brett whispers, 'Eugene hardly ever rings,' while Hilary asks, also whispering, 'How's Wil?'

They adore Wil, and have devised for him a glittering international future. They are gazing at me respectfully, waiting for a reply, when Aunt Gail appears in the corridor, hurrying, raising her hands from her sides, and the twins transfer their adoration to her, and whisper to me, 'Isn't she lovely?'

Aunt Gail is certainly lovely, slim, and bouncy, and fast on her little feet, with some undisguised grey in her fair hair, and so confirmed in her perfect taste that she allows herself the fun of finger-rings galore. As she comes in she flashes those eyes about the room, and without altering her pace takes my bag from the table and swings it to the floor by the side of my chair. 'Cec darling,' she says, 'Nick will be an hour at least. I'll give you a sandwich and some coffee.'

'Let's all have early lunch,' say Hilary and Brett.

But Aunt Gail asks them PLEASE TO LET HER organise this, and tells them that they may have lunch when I am with their father, and that now they can just buzz off. Then the phone rings, and they all close in on it, the twins saying it must be Amy. Aunt Gail gets it, signals that it's for her, and the twins sidle and weave close by, trying to hear what she's saying. It's a very brief conversation, all in second speech mode, with no thumps or runs of emphasis. 'Now COFFEE FOR CEC,' she says as she rings off.

Brett thrusts her face forward and says, 'I bet that was Felix.'

'Never mind.'

'That means it was,' says Hilary.

'Why didn't he turn up?' asks Brett.

Aunt Gail won't answer. She turns away, banging about and making the coffee. I don't know who Felix is. It is likely that I shall never know who Felix is. I only know that he is someone highly desirable, who keeps his options open.

I say mildly to the twins, 'Don't you two ever keep still?'

'They think if they KEEP STILL, they'll GET FAT,' shouts Aunt Gail, without turning round.

We all laugh. The twins run and hug her, and she turns round and struggles out of their grasp and gives me the coffee. 'Now you TWO BUZZ OFF.'

'Where?' they bleat.

'Go and ring Amy,' she says, waving an arm. 'Go on, ring Amy.'

They take oranges from the fruit dish and run

lightly out. 'I haven't the least idea who Amy is,' says Aunt Gail. 'They know about twenty-three Amys. I think it's a generic term for girls who hate the gym teacher. You had better eat something, Cec.'

I shake my head, but she puts a jar of wholemeal biscuits on the table, and I take a few. 'Have you heard from Eugene?' I ask, to get it over.

'I was going TO ASK YOU.' She gives me the wet piteous look. 'He NEVER EVEN RINGS.'

Eugene was her greatest adorer, and had a hard time breaking away. Melbourne was cold turkey for Eugene. 'Maybe,' I say, 'he's too proud to reverse the charges. And biological science's tough. He'll be working like mad for the exams.'

'As YOU SHOULD BE TOO.'

'I did a bit on the train. I can always concentrate on trains.'

'Does HE RING YOU?'

Though I am sometimes seized by fantasy, it's only lately that I've improved at telling the little utilitarian lies. One good thing about Mum, she sensed when I didn't want to tell her something, and didn't ask. Which meant that I didn't get much practice, and have had to learn the hard way that when you must tell lies, don't hesitate. So I don't hesitate. 'Never,' I say.

But the blue eyes are getting their piteous look again, and to keep off the subject of Eugene I say, 'Hey, why did you get all that iron stuff put on the house?'

'Oh Cec, GANGS OF HOONS. From the WESTERN SUBURBS.'

'Watch it,' I say, and she laughs and tells me that I and my kind only alight in the west for a few years, on our way upward, and then, never in the real, the outer west. I shrug and won't answer, because I suspect it's true, and wish it weren't. Sometimes I think I don't want to live anywhere.

'Anyway, how do you know they were from the west?' I ask.

'The ONES WHO WERE CAUGHT WERE.'

And then she says that at least it's not as bad up here as in the Eastern Suburbs, where they snatch your jewellery off you in the street. I put on an amused tolerant look while she gives examples, and when she finishes, I tell her that north, south, east, or west, it's all the same thing, and that they're all hunter-gatherers.

'It works like this,' I tell her. 'The Aborigines were hunger-gatherers, and by stealing their country, and decimating them, and sitting on their heads in various ways, we absorbed practices benign in them but poisonous in us. And thus,' I say grandly, 'the conquerors are conquered.'

'That SOUNDS LIKE CHRIS.'

'No. Me. Though I don't deny the influence.'

'What does WIL THINK OF THAT?'

'He thinks it's poetic.'

'Tactful AS WELL.'

She lets her eyes move over me, abstracted yet thoughtful, and I think she will now say (again) that the marriage clause needn't worry us, not really, because when Wil qualifies, he could do the legal work, and would be sure to win, etc. etc., and then I needn't feel pressured, etc. etc. But instead she suddenly leans across the table and says, quick and fast, 'And what is this question about Chris that Nick can answer and I can't?'

But I've heard all her answers, and they all amount to one thing: golden benign unchanging mother-love. And on would come the wet piteous look, and in reality we would be talking about her and Eugene. So I give little squirms and shrugs and mutter, Oh I don't know, I just thought, and so on. But her eyes stay on me, and I know I must escape before hypnosis takes over. I've finished my coffee, so I put my hand over an orange and ask May I? with my little piggy grey eyes. She waves a hand in defeated assent, and I take the orange, get up, and say in a meek childish voice, 'Please, Auntie Gail, may I go out the back and lie on the grass?'

She waves an arm. 'FEEL FREE.'

The orange is stamped RIVERLAND. I go and sit on a bench on the back terrace and peel its tight skin, using my fingernails and being careful not to break the membrane enclosing those thousands of tiny tear-shaped sacs of juice. 'An orange is a mirac-ulous thing,' Mum would say. 'Look, Cec.' This was when I was small. I would watch closely while she would slowly pull the segments apart and display them as if neither of us had ever seen an orange in our lives before, and then she would pop one segment in her mouth and look ecstatic and incredulous as the juice hit her palate.

'God's own takeaway.'

You would think that someone who loved God's

own takeaway so much would have had a long and healthy life. But there it was, a cancer that started in the breast and was neglected. Was it, I wonder now, because of that marvellous incredulity of hers? because she couldn't believe in that either?

The RIVERLAND orange isn't bad for this time of the year, and as I eat it I look through the big glass doors into the living room. The fortress look hasn't extended to this part of the house, and I can see on the other side the twins huddled over the phone talking to Amy. It's a big room with high ceilings and pale thick sculpted-looking curtains and polished floorboards with rugs and altogether that well-known look of peaceful opulence that Katie and I used to say was the dread and horror of our lives. But now, because at Annandale our yellow cotton blinds are sun-streaked with greyish-white, and there is dust on the tops of our paper moons, and the fronts of our Ikea drawers keep popping out like little awnings and have to be kicked back into alignment, and because I ought to be studying like mad so that one day I'll have a wonderful steady job, and earn enough money to have a room equivalent to that (and then what?) and because I feel sorry for Wil being hampered with someone like me, I feel generally very depressed and hopeless, and wonder if I really want to ask Uncle Nick any questions, or whether I just want him to hug me and massage my scrawny little hands with his.

I put the orange peel in my jeans pocket and go and lie prone on the grass with my head on my arms. The sun penetrates my dry frizzy mousy hair, my spine and my shoulders heat up, and I go to sleep.

Maybe for half an hour. 'Cec, Cec,' I hear, and open my eyes to see four little feet, in plaited leather shoes, trying not to jig. I groan and sit up.

'Cec, Cec, don't tell Mummy this.'

'What?' I say aggressively.

'We've just been telling Amy. We're going to take up the i.'

They show me a page torn from the phone pad.

HILARY EDITH AMBRUSSI

BRETT CHRISTINA AMBRUSSI

'Amy thinks it has panache.'

'When are you going to do this?' I ask.

'In four years.'

'When we're fourteen.'

'What's this about not telling Mummy?'

'When Daddy tried she wouldn't let him.'

'Uncle Ugo picked it up.'

'That's because Italian is the language of music,' I tell them.

'Cec, Cec, what are the Italian Ambrussis like?'

I sit up and rub grass indentations from my fore-arms and mumble that they've seen the photos.

'Yes, but their house and everything.'

'It's all right. It's big. A good bit of gilt.'

'Well, they're Italian,' they say forgivingly, and they start musing over the paper again.

They muse. I stretch. Then suddenly they get clamorous again. 'Cec, Cec, did they like you?'

I shrug, and pretend to consider. 'They were polite.'

Except my great-aunt Antonietta. But the story of my humiliation is not for anybody in this house except maybe for Uncle Nick, if he ever has time to hear it. Gran should have warned me in London, but all she said was, 'Watch out for Etta. She's a bit of a martinet,' and rolled her red-rimmed eyes. Brett is kicking at the grass with a heel and saying, 'Mummy says they're quite nice.'

'We mightn't go to see them,' says Hilary. 'We'll only be on our way to Paris, anyway.'

'Did they offer to put you up?' asks Brett.

'What?' I jump up and whisk grass from my jeans. 'Don't forget,' I say haughtily, 'I was with my friends.'

'With Wil,' they say respectfully. But before their second-hand adoration can develop, Aunt Gail calls my name from the living room door.

'Kindly excuse me,' I say, haughty now to amuse them. 'Good King Nicholas has granted me an audience.'

They are easily amused. They are only ten, after all. I leave them giggling, and go up to the house. Aunt Gail reaches out from the door and puts an arm round my shoulders.

'He's free now, darling,' she says, happy for me. 'And afterwards I'll drive you as far as North Sydney. We're leaving at one-thirty.'

I look at my watch. Ten past one. I say I'll get the train.

'You'll do NO SUCH THING,' she says gaily, and gives my shoulder a squeeze. 'You'll COME WITH US.' And at the same time I hear Uncle

49

Nick say, 'Cecily, my dear.'

He is standing in the door of his new office, a recent addition to the house. Aunt Gail releases me, and as he reaches out and draws me in to that comforting embrace, she dodges around us into the room. Uncle Nick puts his other arm around me, and rests one cheek on my head, and Aunt Gail dodges round us again, and I see, as Uncle Nick releases me, that she is taking out his lunch tray.

I wish I hadn't seen this. She is stumping so fast and humbly away, her back confirming everyone else's busy-ness and my selfish intrusion.

But Uncle Nick is ushering me into a chair, not at his desk, but one of the two leather chairs set apart beside bookshelves, and he is saying calmly, 'We don't see nearly enough of you, Cec. I'm very glad you came.'

He has a soft voice with a slight buzz in it, and his big brown doggy eyes have keen little yellow flecks in them, so that they look gentle and observant at the same time. Without moving this gaze from my face, he says, 'What do you think of my new office?'

I give it a quick survey. It's all absolutely pre-dictable except for the bookshelves to the left of my chair, which is the old scarred one, and is still full of Uncle Nick's collection of books on revolu-tionary history. They aren't in chronological order, and I scan the shelves until I come to the one Eugene and I used to pore over because of the drawing of the young revolutionaries hanging by their necks in St Petersburg Square. I find it between Che Guevara and Fanon. Then I notice, laid flat on top of the shelves, my father's two books, *Sensible Fellows* and *Mr Mother Country*, which I know Uncle Nick has put there so that he can ask if I would like to take them yet. He insists on 'minding' them for me, but can throw them away for all I care. I give a sort of little smile, then survey the room again.

'Good,' I say. 'Logical layout. Wonderful light. But I thought you liked the city office.'

'I'm not severing my ties with Fraser Ambruss just yet, Cecily. Relocation will take a couple of years. But one factor is that most of my clients live up this way, and another is that I've got to establish myself here while I'm still young enough.' He pauses, and looks amused. 'I'm fifty-two, you know.'

I smile, and now that he has put me at my ease, he leans forward, lays both hands gently on my forearms, and says, 'Christina would have been fifty-eight this year.'

'Nobody,' I say, looking at my knees, 'claims she was snatched away in her youth.'

He leans back. 'Cecily dear, Gail says you have a specific question. But first a word about your money. This drop in bank interest? Are you managing?'

'Yes thanks,' I say. 'And Wil and I are working in December. His Mum and Dad can get us work on the western vineyards. Table grapes. They start picking early.'

'That's very hard work, dear.'

'Don't forget we all picked grapes on Crete.'

'That's so, yes. Well, maybe Chris saw the omens when she specified a bank. Maybe. But now, let's get to your specific question.'

Knowing he expects something new, I flush, for my slyness and perfidy. 'I want to know,' I say, looking sideways through the window, 'why she let me go away without telling me she was dying.'

Uncle Nick does not sigh, does not hesitate. 'I thought Gail must have been mistaken when she said it was about Chris, unless you had decided to challenge that marriage clause. But to repeat *that* question, dear, which I did think everyone had taken great pains to answer to your satisfaction.'

I look through the window and say that the satisfaction always melts away, and the question always returns. I make a gesture of despair, bringing my clenched fists down hard on my knees. And then, the next thing I know, Uncle Nick has got up and is standing between me and the window, with one hand cupped loosely in the other at waist level, and is looking as if he is about to address a meeting.

Or a roomful of people after a funeral. Because I remember him standing like that, when I was six, against the windows of Gran's house, after Granddad's funeral, and saying something like, Well, here we all are, all of us who knew and loved him. Then he spoke of Granddad's life, and asked us for our memories of him, glancing at us all but most often at Uncle Ugo, who was sobbing and sobbing as he stood with Gran's arm around him, and with now and again Mum leaning forward to touch his shoulder. He was the only one, apart from me, who didn't contribute his memories: him because of his weeping, and me because it seemed silly at a time like that to talk about Granddad's red waistcoat, which was all I remembered.

And Uncle Nick had stood like that again, with the light behind him again, in Mum's house, or Our House, as I still thought of it then, at the ceremony Aunt Gail arranged for me after I came home. And then I was the one helpless with sobbing, and I refused to be touched by anyone until, after a while, I let Eugene put his hand on my shoulder, and leave it there. The twins and Aunt Gail contributed appropriate memories, and Eugene spoke of her gracefulness, but couldn't get past the word, and kept repeating it, gracefulness, until Uncle Nick nodded, rather sharply, and took over, and after he summed up, and stopped talking, the Doik bird said DOIK, just once.

I stayed alone in the house for a week, stacking possessions and papers and so on, and just when I would feel how silent the house was, and decide that the bird had gone, it would say DOIK, just once. There was a dry spell, and around the house I let the garden die. When I hung a shirt on the clothes line, it would be covered with thrips, and in the mornings they made a dark ring round the seal of the milk bottle. Mum wouldn't use throwaway containers. Mum's two single-mother friends, Sandra and Carmen, rang and offered to come and help, but I said No, and that all I needed was for them to answer my questions. Which they did, patiently and kindly, on the phone, saying what the others said, with variations that led me nowhere. In Mum's desk I found the letters I wrote while away, and made myself read them. I suppose I thought that if I got right down to the depths I would get it over and done with. But they turned out to be mostly stupid drivel, and the one I had absolutely dreaded reading, the one from Lucca, gave only six lines, full of jokes (ha-ha), to my great-aunt's horrible tirade. Also in her desk were my father's two books, which Uncle Nick took for safe-keeping, and the page of information I now call Daddy's Biog. Uncle Nick would come most evenings and drive me over here to dinner, and I would ask the question and howl and carry on, and at night the Doik bird was silent, and I slept fairly well. At the end of the week Wil borrowed a car and drove up to get me, and as soon as I opened the front door we grasped each other, and dropped to the floor of the hall, and had a salty teary fuck. Then we lay on the floor on our backs and looked at the ceiling for ages, and there was absolute silence. It wasn't until we were going down the path to the car, and Wil was saying there was a flat in Annandale he wanted me to see, that the bird said DOIK. I said, 'That's the no-comment bird,' and Wil said, 'Darling, it's one of the wattle birds. This flat is two rooms knocked into one big one, and the light's really good. I knew I was missing you, but I didn't know how much till you opened that door. I love you.' I said, 'I love you too,' and bobbed up and down on the seat of the car, as happy as anything. I wish I had been able just to go on from there, and not to have these fits or bouts of going back, of being forced back, so that now I have to be sitting in this leather chair, looking respectfully but stubbornly at poor Uncle Nick as he begins his address.

'Well, Cecily dear, satisfaction that invariably melts away isn't real satisfaction. I agree with you there. Now, I think we should recapitulate. You have asked that question of how many people?'

And when I don't answer, he says, 'Me. Your Aunt Gail, Chris's doctor, that pair of friends –'

'Sandra,' I say, 'and Carmen.'

'Quite. And Gran on those phone calls to London. So that makes six. And all of us have given you the same answer. Is that right, Cec?'

I say I suppose so, more or less.

'They have all confirmed how much Chris wanted you to have that year, and how well she appreciated the difficulties of getting the six of you together. But that leaves out the most important witness of all, doesn't it, dear? Chris herself. She did say that, didn't she, in the letters you got over there?'

'There was one letter,' I say, 'where she said she was happy I was getting such pleasure and profit from the journey, and she was sure I would never regret taking that year.'

Uncle Nick is nodding. I go on before he can speak. 'That's word-perfect. I know it by heart. If she had said I was *never to regret* taking that year –'

'Splitting hairs,' cries Uncle Nick, trying to laugh.

'No, she was so precise. That would have been an *instruction*.'

'Ha!' says Uncle Nick, triumphant. 'But it would have made you suspicious, knowing she had had that operation. And you would have come home.'

'Would I?'

'Wouldn't you?'

'That's another thing I will never know.'

'Of course you would have. You did know she had had that operation. She did tell you that.'

'Oh yes, and also that cancer wasn't much of a threat these days, and that they were certain they had got it all, and tra-la-la and so on.'

Uncle Nick returns quickly to his leather chair, sits on the edge of it, and takes my forearms in his warm hands. 'Cec, perhaps I've neglected to say that I don't think Christina did the right thing. In fact, I suggested to her in that last month – and I must remind you, dear, that none of us knew until that last month. Not me, not Gail, not Gran –'

'Gran was brought back from London,' I say.

He holds up one hand. 'That was my doing, since it hadn't been specifically forbidden. Let me finish, Cec. Not me, not Gail, not Gran, and not those two friends of hers either. Nobody but her doctor and the visiting nurses knew the truth. But in that last month, when we did know, I put it to her strongly – though naturally inclined to let her have her way at a time like that – I put it to her that you should be brought home. And she pointed out that it was her right to decide, and that Gran and I were not to insult her, nor to treat her like a child, or a doll, by going behind her back. You know how seldom Chris got angry, but when she said that, about being treated like a doll because of her condition, she was angry. And after all that, as you know, none of us was there at the actual time.'

'That was just coincidence. You were all here. All on call. You weren't excluded.'

But now my uncle gives a gasp of grief or fatigue. He releases my arms and leans back in his chair. 'My dear girl, we have been through all this. Surely this isn't what you came up to ask?'

I put a hand on my chest and draw in a deep breath. I feel dried out and angry. 'Did she ever look at *you*,' I ask, 'as if she had never seen you in her life before?'

Uncle Nick laughs in surprise. He jumps to his feet and laughs. 'I had forgotten that. When she was a girl, and I was a little kid, she would suddenly say things like, Look at all this. It is so strange. And it might be the furniture. Or a fence. Always something very familiar. And yes, she would stand there in a kind of, how to describe it, a kind of alert daze, and say, What is it?'

I say urgently, 'But you, Uncle Nick, you. Did she ever look at you like that?'

Uncle Nick shakes his head but then says, 'Yes, wait, once. She picked up my hand.' Uncle Nick is looking at his own hand. 'And said something like, It is so strange. What is it? Yes. And she was made to stop talking like that in front of Ugo, because he would burst out crying.'

'What about you?'

'I forget. I had forgotten the whole thing until you mentioned it. I think it was just an adolescent thing with Chris, you know. It passed.'

'Did it?' I am remembering the oranges. 'I think it was converted into appreciation,' I say, 'and then, maybe, into something else. Because, just before I went away, she would look at me like that, silently, and combined with what she was hiding from me, what she excluded me from, I can't help wondering if that look of hers was, well, if it was dis-dain-ful.'

'Disdainful?' echoes Uncle Nick in dismay.

'Yes, as if she was assessing me, and failing me. Deciding I wouldn't be up to it.'

'Cecily,' says my Uncle Nick, 'Cecily, this is simply another manifestation of your feeling of guilt because you weren't here. It's a transference of your unreasonable guilt.'

I look patient. 'The Parry theory.'

'Edwin Parry is a very good man. You were satisfied at the time.'

'I wanted to be. That's the trouble. I always do. That's why the satisfaction always fades away, and the questions always come back.'

'If you were to return to Mr Parry?' says Uncle Nick.

'It's no good. He didn't know her. You did.'

'True,' says my uncle. 'But our paths diverged. And in these last years there have been the demands of work, not to mention our trouble with Eugene. No, I'm no good, Cec. You should hold onto Mr Parry's conclusion. It's reasonable.'

'I appreciate its neatness.'

'It's more than that,' pleads Uncle Nick. 'More.'

'And it's true I did feel guilty about the fights

Mum and I used to have. But it's not the leaden weight he made it out to be.'

'There are fights in all families,' says Uncle Nick. 'Look at us with Eugene, a boy who had every possible kind of support. And in your case, dear, yours and Chris's, there were, there must have been, strains the, well, the conventional family structures don't have. Oh, but Cecily, what a shame it was, you'll never convince me it wasn't, what a shame about that telephone embargo.'

Uncle Nick and I always disagree about this. If I had rung Mum from somewhere in Europe or India, I don't believe she would suddenly have blurted out the truth. Not after all the trouble she had taken not to. It is a case of Uncle Nick judging his sister by himself. But I don't want to argue about this, nor to say again that Rachel and Wil were under the same embargo, and in a way, we liked it, liked the freedom of it, and certainly understood the economics of it. So I say, 'Well, maybe it was.'

'But that can't be helped now,' says Uncle Nick sternly. He sits down, crosses his legs, and judiciously folds his hands. 'I believe we should look for some particular reason why this thing has recurred just now. The strain of study, perhaps?'

I think of my relaxed scanning of Malory, and want to laugh. But then I say, 'Well, not mine. But Wil's, perhaps, a bit. His family is so poor, and it's so important to him. I don't want to disturb his work mode.'

'That's nice of you,' says my uncle. I notice he looks surprised. 'And it's very like Christina. She didn't want to disturb your travel mode.'

'Neat,' I say. Then because he is getting his hound-dog look again, I lean forward, and put a hand on his, and say, 'Really, honestly, it's not a question of it recurring. I told you, Uncle Nick, it's there all the time, just under the surface, and sometimes it erupts. I try to control it, please believe me, but it gets out of hand. And new explanations keep occurring. For example, yesterday, I thought of indifference. Just that. Indifference. Did she simply become indifferent?'

'Indifferent to you?'

'Indifferent enough to *include* me.'

He stares at me for about five seconds, then he says, 'Well, at least that's trying to see it from her point of view. And that's an improvement, dear, on your attitude so far. So let's keep on doing that, shall we? And ask ourselves if Christina, when she looked at you rather longer than was usual, in that way she had, was only saying goodbye in her own way. That is certainly a possibility, but don't let's rush into saying that it added up to indifference.'

And because he is trying so hard to be patient and reasonable, and because he has given me that image of my young mother picking up her younger brother's hand, and because I feel sorry for him for being badgered by me, but also because I can see, in my mind's eye, the second hand of every watch and clock in this house twitching nervously forward, I say, 'Well, I will really think about that.' Then I (also) pick up one of his hands, and kiss it, and say, 'And you're a good uncle, and always have been.

Thank you for being kind, and letting me talk to you.'

'My dear girl,' he says, 'I wish I could do more.'

My eyes fill with tears, and he leans forward and takes both my hands, and his eyes fill with tears too. 'My dear girl,' he says again.

I disengage my hands and take a tissue from my pocket. As I dry my eyes I hear him say, as if to himself, 'Personally, I believe Chris's doctor should never have told you she knew the worst before you went away.'

And that same old babble of protest starts up in me. I want to shout that if he believes in such blatant deceit, all his comfort is suspect. I pick up my bag and start to get up, but he puts out both hands to stop me. I see that he is heated and agitated, and when there is a knock at the door, he shouts angrily, 'Yes?'

Aunt Gail opens the door, just a bit, and says to him, very gently, 'Shall I ask Sir Roger to come back another time?'

Uncle Nick looks at his watch, hesitates, then jumps to his feet and points dramatically. 'Show him our re-construction of that south-east corner. He wants to see that.'

Aunt Gail doesn't look at me as she very quietly shuts the door. 'Roger has a similar problem in his own garden,' confides Uncle Nick to me.

He is heated and emotional. He sits down, leans close. 'Listen, dear. Now listen. You can help me now. It's about Eugene. You two were so close. We discouraged it, I know, though not for the reason he claimed, it wasn't your, your –'

'My illegitimacy,' I say kindly.

'Ridiculous word, in a time when it's become acceptable, just as Chris predicted it would. But we were blinkered then, I admit it. And there was your youth, too. And first cousins, yes, yes, we did feel it reasonable to oppose it at the time. But there are worse things, as we've learned since. For example – now, listen, dear – did you ever discern in Eugene –' Uncle Nick draws in his chin, so that his eyes look acutely up into mine – 'evidence of homosexuality?'

'Never.' I am shaking my head. Then, in an effort to be fair to Uncle Nick, I stop and think. 'Never,' I say again.

'All the same,' says Uncle Nick dolefully, 'that was years ago.'

My love for Uncle Nick exists outside our differing opinions, but I can't help putting on my tone of innocent amazement. 'And you think he is now?'

He gives a deep sorrowful nod.

'But Uncle Nick,' I say in the same tone, 'why?'

'If he had nothing to hide, why did he go down there and live in poverty and discomfort? And hardly bothers to ring? And answers his mother's letters with a bit of a scrawl on a postcard?' Uncle Nick is speaking very quietly. 'Explain that,' he demands.

But how can I explain without telling him that Aunt Gail was sitting on Eugene's head, and had been sitting on it for as long as Eugene could remember, or as long as I could remember either? I had always supposed that Uncle Nick knew this, and was being silent and loyal about it. Genuinely amazed now, I make myself sound quiet and reasonable. 'Listen, Uncle Nick, Eugene wanted to be independent. That's all. But he needed that. He needed it badly.'

But Uncle Nick is giving me a sad, wise look. 'You weren't here when your Uncle Ugo came to stay. You were in Europe. Now Ugo makes no secret of his preferences. And anyone could see that he took one of his fancies to Eugene. And these days, whenever Gail and I talk it over, we are always forced to the conclusion that it dates from that time.'

'But,' I ask, again with my fabricated amazement, 'on what real evidence?'

'Cecily dear,' he says with dignity, 'this isn't an accusation. It is a loving effort to understand the boy. We are not narrow people. We could adjust to it, I hope. But when it's your own son, dear, your only son, in this time of epidemic. Oh, but at least,' he says, pleading, 'at least, dear, you can assure me that when you and he –'

'I certainly can,' I say, rather loudly.

I wish I had more time to make my ideological position clear, but Uncle Nick looks at his watch again, and then, sighing, almost groaning, presses his knees with both hands as he prepares to get up, as if his joints are suddenly stiff. 'Well, thank you, Cecily,' he says, gloomy and fateful, 'thank you for that. And I don't suppose he rings you, either.'

'Never.' Then I find myself saying (I swear, without premeditation), 'But we know a guy in

Melbourne who knows Eugene, and he says
Eugene has a Chinese girlfriend.'

This is what happens when they don't give you
time to prove something: you have to illustrate it.

'And is really in love,' I say.

Uncle Nick has opened his eyes wide. 'Chinese?'
He takes his chin in a hand. 'Chi-neese.'

'Cantonese, actually.' I rush on, elated. 'Her
name is Chun-Ling. Or at least, that's how it's pro-
nounced. The only thing is, this friend, Ronald,
this friend says she giggles a lot.'

'Giggles.' Uncle Nick's eyes are bright and smiling.
He puts an arm across my shoulders and steers me
towards the door.

'It's only a nervous habit,' I say.

'Of course,' he croons, 'of course.'

'It means you have to take a more sensitive
approach.'

'Of course, I see,' says my uncle, and at the same
time puts a hand on my father's two books, as he
always does, but when I shake my head, as I always
do, he doesn't urge me, but goes on murmuring, 'A
more sensitive approach. Yes, I see. Of course.'

Though his moral opinions divide us, his hug at the
door is as welcome to me as ever. Some people just
have naturally attractive flesh.

'Off you go now, dear, and show yourself to Gail,
and she'll know to send Roger along.'

So off I go, in a bubble of merriment, not quite
dancing. Sir Roger turns out to be a man with a
grey beard, in a grey tracksuit and white Reeboks. As
I approach, his eyes quickly check out my sexual

points. It must be lonely for them working up here, away from the passagiata of the lunch-hour streets and the propinquity of the elevators.

As soon as Aunt Gail sees me, she tells Sir Roger he KNOWS THE WAY, and grabs my arm, and starts to hurry me across the grass.

'We got this appointment AS A FAVOUR.'

She is aiming us at the double gates, through which I see her car waiting in the street. 'I was just telling Uncle Nick,' I say, 'about Eugene's Chinese girlfriend.'

Aunt Gail slows down. 'What Chi-NEESE –'

'A friend of ours in Melbourne told us.'

'WHO IS this friend?'

'Ronald Clark.' As I say this, I realise I took the name from the spine of one of Uncle Nick's books. 'Fairly reliable,' I say.

Aunt Gail is not hurrying at all now. She has released my arm and walks with her head down. 'Chi-neese,' she musingly repeats.

'Cantonese, actually. Her name is Chun-Ling.'

'Marion Wilde has a Chinese daughter-in-law,' muses Aunt Gail. 'So charming and svelte. And,' she adds sternly, 'SO WELL EDUCATED.'

The twins are waiting in the back seat, neat and strapped in. As Aunt Gail and I get in, Brett is saying to Hilary, 'Phoebe is lovely, but she has no character.'

'And of course,' Aunt Gail shouts cheerfully, 'you two have LOADS OF IT.'

They don't bother to reply. I put my bag at my feet. I have come down from my balloon of insouciance and am feeling uneasy about my transference of Sean's girlfriend to Eugene. Not about having done it, exactly, but about having done it so fast and deftly. I am wondering if offering suspect comfort is a family failing, but most of all, I am uneasy about having transferred Chun-Ling's name, and am asking myself if I would have transferred an Anglo name. Or if I would have made one up, picking it up from the spine of a book or a visible object or colour? I say humbly, 'Just drop me at the station, please, Aunt Gail.'

But she shouts WHY, and Hilary and Brett pipe up and say, 'Come with us, Cec. Please, Cec. We want you to.'

I mutter about being able to study well on trains, and about the noise providing the ideal impersonal distraction. I really do want to be alone. I decide that it is all the busy-ness that has hustled me into deceit of that rather elaborate sort. But the twins touch my shoulders and say Please, Please. Those two used to love me when they were little, and there is still a shred or two of affection left over from that time, before they decided that perfection was attainable.

'Of course Cec will come with us,' says Aunt Gail.

She tosses her head, straps herself in, and off we go. Aunt Gail is a notably good driver, and Mum and I both used to remark that after driving for about three minutes, she becomes peaceful. Mum said that the management of the powerful car evidently satisfied the need she usually expressed in all that shouting and metaphorical pointing, so that while driving with Aunt Gail, you could usually count on second speech mode being maintained.

I look at the helpless-looking little white hands on the big wheel, at the rings on her pointed fingers, and remember Eugene and me when small, hanging about her, touching those rings, adoring.

At that stage Gene and I tended to worship as a pair, another object of this welded admiration being Uncle Ugo after Granddad's funeral. Turning away from that gentle face, that intimate voice, we each saw our charmed state reflected in the other's eyes. A few years later, we would call this our shared magnetic field.

As soon as I see that Aunt Gail has settled into her emotionally sedated state, I say that nobody told me that Gene was in Sydney last year. 'Or that Uncle Ugo was in Sydney, and stayed with you.'

She replies that nobody intended to keep it secret. She is calm but dismissive. I turn my head and incline an ear to the twins. 'Did you like Uncle Ugo?'

I detect caution in their reply. Yes, they say, they did. 'But he isn't really famous,' adds Hilary.

'You see his photograph on CDs though,' says Brett.

'Never at the front,' says their mother serenely to the road.

Both twins lean forward in their straps, aim their faces at their mother, and tell her that she's just repeating what Uncle Ugo said himself.

'Those were his exact words,' says Brett. 'Never at the front.'

'But sometimes inside,' says Hilary, 'with his head the size of a pea. We were eating peas, Cec –'

'Yes, Cec, and he picked up one and then ate it and said, Off with his head.'

The twins giggle. Then Brett aims her face at her mother's back again and says, 'Ye-es, and he and Gene played our recorders in the garden all night.'

'It was not all night,' says Aunt Gail. 'Daddy had to go out and put a stop to it. We have neighbours to consider.'

While the twins mutter that recorders aren't loud, I say I have only met Uncle Ugo once, and was looking forward to seeing him in Europe. 'I hoped so much he would be in London with Gran, or that I could make a detour to Paris or somewhere.'

'Paris,' repeated Aunt Gail, on a little laugh.

'But it turned out he was nowhere in Europe. He was in America.'

'South America,' said my aunt.

'And here, don't forget,' said Brett from the back. 'At the Opera House.'

'The Town Hall,' says her mother.

'I remember him,' I say, 'as so charming.'

'Oh he is,' says Aunt Gail. 'He takes great pains. But he's a fiddle player in the low to middle rank. And that's the fact of the matter.'

The twins demur, and name a quartet or two, but they are so uncertain of their facts that Aunt Gail easily quells them by saying pleasantly, 'So let's have no more nonsense about fame and genius and so on.'

She takes one of those powerless-looking hands from the wheel and waves to a grey-haired woman walking two dogs. Hilary pushes across Brett and they both eagerly wave too.

'There's Mrs Parker. Isn't she lovely?'

Mrs Parker is another person whose identity I am content never to discover. Possibly she is Felix's mother. The twins settle into an infatuated discussion on Jack Russell terriers, and Aunt Gail says to me, 'Was Nick able to answer your question?'

'Up to a point,' I reply politely.

'I'm so glad. But it does seem to be a serial process. I sometimes wonder if this re-location will be successful. It certainly won't unless it's understood that an office is a place of business.'

'I know. I'm sorry. I just got desperate when you said I couldn't come on Saturday.'

'But Cec,' she says, amazed, 'we agreed on Saturday.'

'Only if you rang first.'

'I must have given you the wrong impression, Cec.'

From the back I hear, Oooo. But Aunt Gail presses on. 'I'm so sorry if I did that, Cec, if I gave you the wrong impression. You must be very confident about your exams, Cec.'

'Reasonably confident. I need to do some reading in Malory.'

'I know you're good in English, but over-confidence is a danger. It's clever of you not to disturb Wil, anyway. I've yet to meet a poor lawyer.'

We are passing swiftly through Turramurra, on

the altered and memory-free highway. I say I don't know if Wil wants to practise law. There have been so many scams and scandals involving Sydney lawyers that I need to say this, and am sorry that it comes out sounding so prim and poncy. 'Legal history,' I say, 'is Wil's particular interest.'

She asks, with a hint of alarm, 'Then will he teach?'

The twins are silent. I sense their attention. 'Oh,' I say, in a rising voice, 'I don't know. How would I know? I don't know what I will do, either. I don't know anything.'

'Who does?' asks my aunt-by-marriage humorously. 'But in the meantime, wouldn't it be just as well if you were to get a really good pass in your exams, and let other considerations wait?'

I can't think of an answer that isn't too boring to make. We drive in silence for a while, when Aunt Gail says, 'You made a very good impression on Gran, anyway.'

'Did I?' I say, sulking.

'Yes, I assure you. And Wil. She loved Wil.'

'I expect she told you that,' I say, 'when she was brought back to Sydney because she was told about Mum.'

'Don't be like that, dear,' says Aunt Gail in a low voice.

'And while I was still away, because I wasn't.'

'Hush. Please.'

But of course, the twins have heard. 'Gran stayed with us for ten days,' says Hilary.

'We quite liked her,' says Brett.

'She said she would put us up when we go to London.'

'Not if Ugo is in residence,' says their mother. She pitches her voice very low. 'Cec, do you remember Chris saying that doting always has a victim?'

I mutter yes. The words, suddenly recalled, are so clear that I wonder what else I have forgotten.

'It's discourteous to whisper,' accuses Brett.

'It's only something about Gran,' says Hilary.

'Where are my specs?' cries Hilary in a high quavering voice.

'And my purse. You two, where are my specs and my purse?'

The twins collapse into giggles. Aunt Gail says equably, 'Wait till you're eighty-two.'

They control their giggling for long enough to cry out, 'Fruit and veg have been good to us,' before they collapse into another fit, out of which Hilary wails, 'That was when we still had a stall in the old markets.'

'Before they moved out to Homebush,' sobs Hilary.

'Oh, you wretched girls,' says their mother.

But she is smiling herself, and so am I.

The twins calm down. They wipe their eyes. They say again that they quite liked Gran. 'Only,' says Brett suddenly, 'I can't stand to look at her droopy cheeks.'

'Can't stand looking at,' says Aunt Gail.

'Looking at, then,' says Brett morosely.

'Or can't bear to. Honestly, Cec, the things they pick up at their supposedly good schools.'

'Well, I can't' says Brett. 'Or her droopy old red eyelids either.'

'Gran can't help it,' says Hilary, with subdued gloom.

'If you ask me,' says Brett, 'Aunt Chris was lucky.'

'And if you ask me,' says Aunt Gail promptly, 'you had better shut up. Sorry, Cec.'

'It's okay.' I turn my head to give the twins a reassuring look, then wonder if it is not also complicitous. I wonder if I have really taken Mum's advice and reasoned myself out of my dismay at the sight of old women. This was when I used to see them getting out of coaches at motels, or coming out of their clubs, or centres, or whatever they call them. 'It wouldn't be so bad,' I said to Mum, 'if they didn't get around in gangs.'

She asked me what I expected them to do, since most were widows, and their families dispersed or working. 'Do you want them to stay home alone?'

'Yes,' I said, 'and be wise and philosophical.'

I was only ten.

She laughed, but then said, 'Now look, that's fear you feel. That's primitive fear. Face it. Use your reasoning faculties.'

So I did that. I faced it. I used my reasoning faculties. But occasionally the old dismay still takes me by surprise, pouncing before I can repress it.

In the back of the car, the twins are silent and morose, each looking through different windows. Aunt Gail is steady and peaceful. When Hilary languidly asks her for the Vitamin E cream, she takes a tube from the glove box and passes it in silence over her shoulder. In the rear view mirror I watch Hilary's slender little hands lovingly administer to each other. In silence we pass through Gordon and Killara. But as we come into Lindfield, I hear from the twins a sudden and intense whispering. This turns out to be like the sizzle before fireworks, because then they thrust their faces forward and shout together.

'Mummy-Mummy, we can buy it in there.'

'I can't park here,' says Aunt Gail.

'You can, you can. Round that corner.'

'Mummy-Mummy, you promised.'

'You promised. You promised. You did, you did.'

'Well,' says Aunt Gail crossly, as she turns the corner, 'there's just time, I suppose.' She draws into the curb and says, as they tumble out, 'But only if you hurry. Go on. Hurry. Run. Run.'

Through the window I see a sign forbidding parking at any time. 'Oh God,' says Aunt Gail, 'that's exactly what I need now. A ticket. And I must say, Cec, that I still don't understand what Nick can tell you about Chris that I can't. In fact, I was much more involved than Nick was. I did her shopping, YOU KNOW THAT, right up to the time she went into that place.'

I look through the window and say, 'I know,' though it is not true. The squares on Mum's kitchen calendar showed 'G – shopping p.m.' on eight or nine dates, but after that it was always S or C, and I knew that Sandra had driven up in her big pink car, with fins, or that Carmen, who has ascended in the world of business, had come over in her fast efficient car. I don't quite know why I never confront my uncle's wife with her deceits. It feels like a mixture of fear and hopelessness, with an occasional suspicion that nobody could be so brazen if they were not also self-deceived. I dropped that kitchen calendar into a carton with an egg-slice and a frying pan, both with charred handles, and the dishcloths dried hard in their twists. 'I know,' I say, to Aunt Gail, 'but Uncle Nick knew her longer, and can answer other things.'

She is looking at me with her lips pursed. 'Do you ever ask yourself WHY ARE YOU SO SELF-ABSORBED?'

'Quite often,' I say, to shut her up.

'You haven't EVEN ASKED ABOUT my exciting news.'

'I'm sorry, Auntie,' I say meekly. 'What is it?'

'I am to STAND FOR PARLIAMENT.'

I am not really surprised. I know that after feminism Aunt Gail was active in urban conservation, and that she was, and perhaps still is, on the local council. I smile and say, 'That's marvellous, Aunt Gail. That's a really good idea.' I mean this. I believe it. If she uses her power there, she might lay off everybody else. 'State parliament?' I ask.

'My dear, I'm not TAKING ON THE FEDS YET.'

She will stand as an Independent, she tells me, and names an electorate. Then she tells me that the retiring member is Jim Canning, and that she used to go to school with his sister Kirsty. There have been dinners, she says, and it was lovely to meet Kirsty again, after all these years. And Kirsty's husband, too, Vernon Huth.

Vernon Huth is my father, and this Kirsty must be his third (or, for all I know, his fourth) wife. I turn my head and look through the window.

'Vernon is surprised,' I hear her say, with an amazing touch of trepidation, 'that you haven't been to see him.'

'Oh?' I say. 'Why?'

'He DID ASK YOU TO. Or so I gathered.'

'If that's what you gathered,' I say, 'he's a liar as well. I still have his letter. It was a fence of spikes.'

'People can have SECOND THOUGHTS. And,' says my aunt-by-marriage, 'Kirsty is A SWEET THING.'

'You mean she might have sweetly persuaded him to see me.'

'Cec, the WAY YOU SAY THAT.'

'How many children have he and this sweet Kirsty had?'

'None,' says my aunt shortly.

'Oh well,' I say, 'I suppose since he had about a hundred already.'

'You are SO SILLY.'

'How many then?'

'Ask him yourself.'

'Fat chance.'

'He would LOVE TO SEE YOU.'

I reach for my bag, but before I can proclaim that I'll get the train from Lindfield station, thank you, and goodbye, goodbye, she says, 'Eugene saw him quite recently, when Vernon went to Melbourne for something or other.'

I am arrested, my hand on my bag. 'How do you know, if Gene never rings?'

But she gives this one of her fast dismissals, with just a touch of scorn to make you feel stupid for having asked. 'Oh, this was WEEKS AGO.' And at the same time the twins run up from behind and start scrambling into the car, one of them flapping a big magazine about, and Aunt Gail turns her head and yells at them that it's HIGH TIME TOO.

And after all, if I stay where I am, I'll get home sooner, and shall ring Eugene's friend Angelo straight away, and ask him to tell Eugene to ring me, so that I can put him in the picture about his Chinese girlfriend. Yes. And also, I shall have time to go out and buy food for dinner. I want to do this because at present Wil is financially low, and if we eat out, there will be tension about me paying, and Wil is likely to get proud, etc.

As we join the traffic, Aunt Gail tells me please TO THINK ABOUT IT, and that I REALLY SHOULD. I ignore this, and the twins, huddled over the glossy magazine across their laps, are incurious for once. Then we are moving fast and steady in the traffic, and Aunt Gail and I are chatting about this and that. I have the same old tumult of undirected protest working in me, but it doesn't stop me from chatting about this and that, or rather, to respond to Aunt Gail by murmuring:

'Really.'

'That's interesting.'

Or, for a change of texture, 'I wonder if I really agree.'

Somewhere in this inane exchange she manages to insert the information that Vernon and Kirsty have had a terrible time with that house at Coogee. 'Really?' I say from my remote place. 'How interesting.'

We catch all the green lights, and at North Sydney station I gallop down those hundreds of steps bursting with the joy of release plus a bit of self-congratulation because I've done better than usual (though not really well) in the matter of resisting hypnosis.

I make a split-second connection with the train, a glassy Tangara this time, which groans as it opens its doors, and when I've come up the steps at Town Hall, I see one of the westie buses across George Street, and I run across, just as the light changes to red, and hop on.

So when I turn into our street, it's only half past two. The renovators' truck is outside our building, but I don't hear any drilling.

I don't even notice the fuggy air.

In the letter box I find a card from Katie. From Turkey. Turkey! I flick a look at the stamp, and notice that the writing space is fairly densely filled, but as I walk up the steps I look only at the picture, which is of the tiles in the mausoleum of Sultan Suleyman. The steps are covered with coarse dust from the renovation. I unlock the door and carefully, ritualistically, place the card, picture-side up, on my end of our work table, saving it for after I've rung Angelo.

Exactly at that moment, the drills start up. I shout Shut up at the top of my voice. Then I get a padded quilt from the cupboard and put it over my head, making a tent which contains me and the phone. I grab an ear plug, stuff it into one ear, and ring Angelo.

Angelo said he would leave a note on Eugene's door.

So I am waiting for Eugene to ring.

And can't go out to buy food in case he does.

When Eugene rings, I'll ask him to hang up, then ring him back, because he's so poor, and it's prime time, and it may take me a while to explain about his Chinese girlfriend.

Poverty, as Mum used to say, is relative. Gran always tells me to hang up, then rings me back.

I feel slightly nervous about explaining to Eugene about his Chinese girlfriend, but count on our shared magnetic field, which wobbled when we were lovers, but after that returned (almost) to its childhood steadiness.

This is not the kind of waiting I hate. The drills have stopped, and the tapping noises sound preoccupied and peaceful. I've opened all the windows. They click slightly because they are loose in their frames. I've had a shower and washed out my Indian shirt which is now suspended from the travelling clothes line we pull out between two hooks, and whenever I look at it I see it waving its arms at me in a languid yet spirited way.

The kind of waiting I hate is the kind Katie inflicted. I hereby state that I hate waiting: 1, in the street; 2, in foyers of cinemas after the film has started; 3, alone in coffee shops and cafes.

Katie's card contained nothing, basically, except that she is travelling with an American news photographer forty-five years old, and that the bells are ringing. And then some remarks about cold autumn winds. Yes, actually, the weather.

Katie's card is also full of dashes and exclamation marks, such as: Long letter soon – Promise!!!

I do not intend to encourage in myself the suspicion that there is something spiteful about all these dashes and exclamation marks, because to do so would be to ignore the possibility that Katie has genuinely changed, and is not just getting at me, and pointing out how prissy I am, which she sometimes used to do. She also says, in a postscript: Mum says you've been ringing. Which made me feel as if I had been nagging, which she once accused me of (waving her arms and talking about the middle classes) when finally she did turn up, an hour late.

As I turned Katie's card back to Suleyman's beautiful tiles, I thought of all the moribund quarter, half, and whole hours I've spent waiting for Katie, and then I thought of all the little seeping of my mind waiting for Katie to write. And it came to me that I have finished with Katie.

And it is a relief. I hereby state that it is a true relief, and not just disguised anger. And also that I realise I am mostly to blame, for my stupid expectations.

Goodbye, Katie. I release you from my stupid expectations.

I put the card, writing side up, on Wil's end of the table, for him to read when he gets home. Usually I would have kept it at this end, my end, and given it to him from here.

The paper in these airmail pads is nearly as thin as the paper Katie and I used to use in high school for rolling joints, but is much firmer and finer of texture. I bought the first pad in Verona, then ran back the next day and bought five more. But I was manic about keeping down the weight of my pack, so I kept two for current notes and posted the others back by surface mail to Mum, saying two for you and two for me. They took months to arrive. I found them thrown on the front verandah at Turramurra on the exact day I reached the last page of the last one I kept. And in that week of the Doik bird, that was the most consoling event.

Wil and I never hide any letters, diaries, notes etc. from each other. Now and again, when I'm here at our work table alone, I've been tempted to pick up and read a letter from his family. They live on the North Coast, and he has a sister and two brothers, all younger than him. They usually keep in touch by phone, but sometimes his mother writes him a letter, and lately his younger brother, Ed, has taken to writing him eight-page letters, wild and disjointed with complaint. Wil gives me a summary of his family letters, including Ed's, as he reads them, so I don't expect to uncover anything private when I have this temptation. So it is, I suppose the epitome of Idle Curiosity. It shames me, because I think of it as typical of women of former times, who seem to me to have been a sneaky lot, and it wouldn't even be worth thinking about if it didn't illustrate the difference between me and Wil, who I am sure is never even slightly tempted to sneak a look at anything of mine.

Does that mean that Wil is less interested in me, on that level, than I am in him? Probably. And does that matter? The fact that I can even ask that last question means I've changed since that night in the Min'h Hai.

All the same, in spite of my trust in Wil, or in his lack of interest, I always put these personal pads, once I've filled them up, right at the bottom of my pile of books. Why? There isn't anything in them I want desperately to hide from Wil, and besides, all my space-saving symbols and abbreviations would make reading them hard labour. In fact, I can hardly read some of them myself, and if I don't take the time to capture them fairly soon, all will be lost. If that matters. No, I hide them either because I am instinctively sneaky, or because if I knew he read them, I would write them in a slightly different way, and they would stop being MINE.

I hid things from Mum too. Gran, who definitely comes from a sneaky generation, and probably recognised another sneak when she saw one, once gave me a small filing case with a lock and key, and I used to file Eugene's letters and my dancing clothes under ENVIRONMENT. My dancing clothes fitting easily into an A4 manilla envelope. I would put them on under a cotton dress or my school overcoat and stroll out calling good-by-eee. I must have filed them like that for the pleasure of secrecy (to keep them MINE) because, although Katie used to say that you can never tell with mothers, I didn't doubt then, and I don't now, that she respected my privacy.

I still use that case. The papers I found in Mum's desk are filed there. Her letters, her and my birth certificates, and that single page headed: DETAILS, POSSIBLY USEFUL, ABOUT YOUR FATHER.

She used to try to tell me these details, but as she had already told me of his refusal to take any interest in me, I refused to take any interest in him, and wouldn't listen. So she was reduced, as she wrote beneath that heading, to writing them down.

As my attempts to inform you of these
details invariably lead to estrangement, I am
reduced to writing them down.

Or words to that effect.

When I was expecting Vernon Huth to reply to Uncle Nick's letter, I did get out that page and read it. But when he actually did reply, I put it back.

'Daddy's biog,' I said to Wil, giving the case a kick.

'Good,' said Wil, approving not of the kick, but of my filing it away. I suppose he thought I would tear it up. So he said, approving, Good.

I could almost see Mum approving Wil's approving. Sometimes I feel those two have me caught in a pincer movement. There's no doubt that they liked each other. They met only once, but she seemed to

like him spontaneously, as well as doing her mad-
dening assessment act on him and telling me afterwards that he had a well-shaped head, and well-set
ears, and candid eyes and so on.

'What are his parents like?' she asked.

'Look, Mum,' I said, with my parody of patience.
'Wil and I are friends, right? We're not about to get
married or anything.'

'You're about to travel together.'

'Yes, that's right, Mum. And there will be six of us,
remember?'

'Please Cecily,' she said, 'not the teenage soapie
style again.'

About a year before this, we had had a show-
down, a really intense quarrel, about the way I
treated her with false patience, with soft hopeless
sighs and half-hidden smiles. She had made me
admit the injustice of this standardised style. I had
realised its insultingness, also (her words) its imagi-
native poverty, and had tried to abandon it. But I
must have needed it, or felt I did, because I would
still fall into it when I felt defensive, or anxious
about her opinion.

So I said patiently, 'But Mum, what does it
matter what his parents are like?'

'You've met them?'

'Once.'

'Please give me your impressions.'

'But why? Why?'

'Oh, be generous.'

It was one of those occasions I remember clearly.
Wil and I had been lovers for months, but it wasn't

until our journey looked feasible at last that parents were brought into it. So that was his first (and only) visit. We had tea at the big table on the verandah, on the end that wasn't occupied by gardening gear, and Mum and Wil were doing most of the talking, mainly about travel, Wil saying how tough it was to choose a destination, because to choose one meant to abandon another, and Mum claiming as a consolation that only the places we fail to reach remain intact. They retain, she said, their ideal essence. After an hour or so I went inside and made lunch and coffee and brought it out, and now Wil and Mum were talking about the Ambrussi family at Lucca, and how she had stayed with them to give English lessons to her cousin Carla.

'A Catholic family, of course, especially the older members. In fact, Carla and I had to develop strategies to keep Carla's mother off the subject of my father's apostasy. She must have been pleased when he slipped back in, belatedly though it was. I wanted to ask Carla about that, about her mother's reaction, but our correspondence had petered out onto postcards by that time. Sad. We had all those sisterly jokes. On the last card, however, she did say that Cec would be welcome to call.'

'It came over as a bit stiff to me,' I said.

'Possibly,' said Mum. 'But do go. It's a chance to see the Italian borghesia at home. They aren't eager to let you in. Not unless they have something to gain, such as English lessons.'

'All that might have changed,' said Wil.

'Possibly. But they're a very practical people.

Why not? They've been invaded so often, trampled over so often.'

When Wil left, I walked with him for a couple of blocks down the street, and then, because we were deep in talk, for a few more. And when I went back to the house, and was passing the door of her office, she called me in. I was expecting it, because I had heard the noise of her work stop as I approached, and knew what was coming, and thought I might as well get it over and done with. Her desk was set sideways, in full view of the door. She was sitting at her word processor, and had paused in the middle of someone's thesis or manuscript or whatever. Her feet were hooked far back on the struts of the chair, her back was straight, and she didn't take her hands off the keyboard. She asked her questions about Wil's parents almost sternly, but when she said, Oh, be generous, she smiled.

So, struggling against the soap, I told her I liked Wil's parents, then, after more interrogation on her part, and more or less soap on mine, I told her they had been late-sixties drop-outs. At first I made them out to be hippies, because it was easier (soapier) but then explained that they had adopted a frugal and self-reliant rural lifestyle in revolt against consumerism and all that. (I knew this would please her because she was so frugal herself, not only from necessity, but as a principle.) But, I told her, the economics of the thing meant that they would do an injustice to their clever children, and so they had climbed painfully into society again, and were still paying off a newsagency. I told her that Wil admired them for that, since they had never lost their early ideals, and still spoke with longing of that time.

She said lightly, 'Ah, homesickness.'

'Yes,' I said, though I knew nothing about home-sickness at that time. Then, in case I was making them sound too wonderful, I said that in some ways they were still unreconstituted sixties types, and said shit and fuck all over the place.

She smiled and said that people who said fuck pejoratively, yet professed to value the act so much, always seemed to her to be taking the name of the Lord their God in vain. This made me furious, because she had said it before, and I hated it when she repeated herself. She hadn't taken her hands off the keyboard. 'But at least,' she said, 'they're not likely to object to your illegitimacy.'

I went into pure soap, and gave one of my long patient sighs.

'Stop it,' she said. 'Does Wil know who your father is?'

Though Wil knew quite a bit about Vernon Huth (having known a few of his students), I gave another of my hopeless sighs. 'I was crazy to ask him home,' I said. 'I knew I shouldn't have. I knew.' And then, I remember, she gave a sudden, broad, bright smile, and said, almost singing, 'All right. It's all right,' and before I got out of the room her word processor was going as if it had never stopped. It seems strange now to think that as she sat there, giving that sudden smile, she must have known that she was unlikely to survive.

She had to work fairly hard. Granddad was so affronted by my existence that Gran could hardly ever persuade him to see her, or me. And though he let her live in the house, she had to keep it in repair, and pay the rates, and keep us both. I got jobs waitressing or on checkouts in school holidays, but it was Gran who sent the money for my year of travel.

Wil liked Mum, too, though he said he hadn't imagined her like that. As I walked those blocks of the street with him, he kept giving me little fresh alert glances, as if seeing her had made him see me in a new light. He said he had known she was quite old, and had that marvellous tall figure, but that he hadn't imagined her as so pedantic. Well, he said, almost prim. I said she wasn't prim, but had a kind of scrupulousness that could be off-putting. I also said that one day, he would see that she could burst into such wild and funny moods that she didn't seem like the same person. But as it happened, he never saw her like that. And as it happened, neither did I, again.

I suppose I was pleased they liked each other, and kept asking me questions, but sometimes it made me a bit hostile, or impatient. He asked why, with her intelligence, and the money in the family, she wasn't equipped to do more interesting work than copying. And I had to explain that in the fifties it was fairly common for girls to get hooked on travel, really addicted, and just to become hot-shot typists and work their way round the world. And now, I said, she loved the freedom of working in her own time and her own way and her own clothes, and wouldn't change it for anything. That's what she had told me, and that's what I passed on to Wil when he asked. And when she said, about him, that though he was so conspicuously handsome, he did have, slightly, ever so slightly, the worn look she had seen in very young fishermen and farm labourers in poor countries, I had to explain that as the eldest child, he had played a part in his parents' climbing back in, and about the paper deliveries, and all that. And she said, well, that worn look was reversible, sounding so soothing that I had to say coldly that I didn't mind in the least if it wasn't.

She was right. It was reversible. But because she pointed it out, I occasionally see evidence of it. I have never mentioned it to him, of course. I've never told him how much I like this difference between him and those guys who have always lived the Fat Life, which is, of course, another of her terms.

Eugene didn't ring till five o'clock. And it turned out that he hadn't been home, hadn't seen Angelo, but had just decided, on impulse, to ring me from a pay phone in the street. I took for granted that, as usual, he was going to say, it is still you, Cec, it is only you. So I get reproachful in advance.

'Oh, Eugene, this is prime time.'

But he says loudly that he doesn't care. He sounds a bit drunk. 'Gene darling,' I say, 'give me a number where I can ring you back.'

'No,' he says, 'I won't. And don't worry about the money. A guy just gave me back twenty bucks I lent him. When we were both fifteen, for God's sake. And I've got something to tell you.'

I start to say I've got something to tell him too, but he won't listen. 'This guy who gave me back the money, he saw your father last week.'

'Really,' I say coldly.

'Here, in Melbourne, in the street. And do you know what he was doing.'

'Pissing on a lamp post,' I say.

Eugene gives a shout of laughter. Behind him a tram passes, ringing its bells. 'No, truly, Cec,' he says then, 'I'll tell you. He was walking over Princes Bridge. And he had on an executive suit, real sharp, padded and pressed and all, and a felt *hat*, with a band and all. And was carrying a brief-case. And had bare feet. Bare feet. Walking fast. Absolutely composed.'

I am silent, but intent.

'This guy said it was marvellous. And a gang of guys following. Everybody laughing.'

'Yes?' I say reluctantly.

'Except him, except him,' clamours Eugene. 'See? Absolutely composed everyday face. Which made it. See?'

'Yes,' I say reluctantly.

'And,' says Eugene, 'this guy says he has real pretty pearly little feet.'

I sit on the edge of the bed. I feel slightly breathless. 'Eugene,' I say, 'now I want to tell you something.'

'Wait on. Wait till I tell you one more thing.'

'Please don't, Eugene.'

'No, wait on. Wait, Cec, listen. I've got a girl.'

'Gene,' I say, going floppy in the shoulders. 'You mean you love her?'

'You told me it would happen. And it has. I love her, Cec.'

'Well,' I say, 'I am so glad.'

This is probably true. But if I am glad, I am also confused, because I can't think how I can wheedle my confession into this conversation. 'She isn't,' I hear myself saying helplessly, 'Chinese, by any chance?'

There is a pause. Then just as I am about to explain my question by confessing, he says curtly, 'Why do you ask that?'

I wave my free arm. 'Oh, please, not because of any racist –'

But he interrupts, still curt. 'Come on, Cec. Who told you?'

'Wait,' I say. 'Now wait. She *is* Chinese?'

'Who told you?' Eugene still sounds belligerent. If we were speaking face to face, he would be bucking his head. 'Come on, Cec. Who told you?'

'Ronald Clark,' I say, in a dream.

'Who the hell's he? I wanted to tell you myself. What *is* all this, Cec?'

'Wait,' I say. 'Is she Cantonese?'

'No.' He is still belligerent. 'She's Australian. Fifth generation Australian. Born right here in Melbourne. Her name's Susan. Susan Wu.'

'I don't believe this,' I say.

'You had better believe it. I'm bringing her home for Christmas. I'm going to ring Dad and ask him for our plane fares.'

'You'll get it,' I say.

'You think?'

'I think.' It has dawned on me that I need not make my confession now. I can postpone it, even, till we are both quite old. And in the meantime, it can just be assumed that Ronald Clark has got his Chinese girlfriends confused. 'In fact,' I tell Eugene, 'they may be pleased.'

'They had better be,' says Eugene. 'She'll be their daughter-in-law.'

'What?' I say. 'Legal and everything.'

'Eventually. There's her family, you see, Cec.'

'And that's fine with you?'

'Everything's fine with me, Cec. And that's the truth.'

'Oh, Gene. Describe her, Gene.'

'Aaah,' says Eugene adoringly. 'Aaah. Well, I'll tell you. She just looks so marvellously uncomplicated and bloody peaceful-looking. You know what her head's like?'

'Her head? No.'

'A brown egg. Now what could be more uncomplicated and peaceful-looking than a brown egg?'

I sigh jealously. 'I see what you mean. Economy of design.'

'Exactly. None of that Caucasian wastefulness. Same thing with her body.'

'No Anglo lumps and bumps.'

'But wait on, Cec. This is the best part. This is the

part you'll like. Her father –'

Eugene collapses into laughter. 'Go on, go on,' I shout, laughing myself. 'Her father?'

'Her father,' says Eugene, crowing, 'has a stall in the markets.'

I collapse backward on the bed. 'Not,' I say, and gasp and crow and yell, 'Not – a – stall –'

'In the markets,' shouts Eugene. 'Fruit and –'

'Fruit and veg have been good to them,' I shout back.

'It's dyn-as-tic, dyn-as-tic –'

We are both gasping and laughing and saying dyn-as-tic, and I'm lying back across the bed waving my legs like a beetle, when Wil comes in. As he passes I stretch out my free hand to him, and he shakes it solemnly, then goes and puts his bag on the floor under his side of our work table.

'Enough-enough for now,' I say in sing-song to Eugene. 'I'll get in touch after the you-know-whats.'

'How's your work going for those?'

'Fine,' I say, drawling. 'Just fine.'

'Mine too,' he says, in the same bored tone. He and I decided to oppose exam fever at the same time, when we were thirteen. 'Susie's is too,' he adds.

'What's she doing?'

'Same as me,' he says, as if I should know this.

'Longing to meet her.' I am watching Wil pick up Katie's card. 'Goodbye, Gene darling.'

'Goodbye, Cec love.'

But somewhere beneath this conversation, I must have been ruminating. Because suddenly I say, 'Wait, Gene, wait. Where were his shoes?'

'His shoes? Whose shoes? Oh, *his* shoes?'

'Yes. Where were they?'

'I don't know, Cec,' says Gene, in an injured tone.

Then we have to say good-bye again. And then I sit up on the edge of the bed and smile peacefully across at Wil. 'Eugene,' I say.

'I gathered.' He puts down Katie's card. 'Typical Katie.'

'Yes. Goodbye, Katie.'

He gives me a curious look, but only says, 'We never got to Turkey.'

'So it remains intact.'

But Wil is too tired to respond to this reminder of Mum's opinion that only the places we fail to reach remain intact. When Wil is very tired, he goes white, and a blue-grey triangle fans out from the inner corner of each eye. 'It was either India or Turkey,' he says, and picks up Katie's card, and throws it down again.

I get up and wind my arms round him and put my head against his chest. He embraces me with one arm, and lightly kisses me. But he is warning me by his slight resistance, also his forbearance. As I let him go I remember Aunt Gail saying, 'Tactful AS WELL.'

'No other mail?' he asks.

I shake my head. 'You were expecting something?'

'Dreading is more like it. I rang Mum from the library. Ed didn't come home at all last night.

Twelve years old. It could have been anything. And then this morning he turns up and locks himself in his room.'

'He's just inflicting the usual torture,' I say. I am about to add that I often wonder why anyone has children, but as this is too rich a topic to embark on at present, I say instead, 'Eugene's fallen in love.'

'Good for Eugene.' Wil looks at me with his head tilted. 'And it lets you off the hook.'

'You mean it lets him off the hook.'

'Both of you then. Was the noise bad today?'

'Not too bad.'

The moment I say this, I know that I don't intend to mention that I was absent for most of the day, nor that I went up to talk to Uncle Nick. It isn't that I want to deceive Wil, but that I am overwhelmed by the need to make my motives comprehensible, while at the same time negotiating the barrier, or black rock, of his preoccupation. It isn't that I don't long to tell him about it. I do. It presses me. But it doesn't lend itself to a quick summary. In fact, it would be easier, though I suppose no more comprehensible, to dance it.

The sleeves of my Indian shirt give me an insouciant wave. I catch it by a cuff. It is dry. Nor shall I tell Wil about my father's feet, nor that Eugene's girl is Chinese, nor that her father is in fruit and veg, nor why I am finished with Katie. I haul the shirt down and say, 'Sometimes there's no drilling. Just light tapping. But it's unpredictable.'

'Shit,' says Wil, depressed. 'Well, I've got to shower.'

While he showers, I put on the Indian shirt and brush my hair. Giving up on explanations has let a lovely lazy feeling in. When Wil comes out of the shower, the grey triangles less noticeable, and his thick chestnut hair, so adored by the twins, standing up straight from his white brow, I relent enough to say, 'Eugene's girl is Chinese.'

'So,' says Wil, and smiles, but then looks worried. 'We've got to make a point of ringing Sean and Chun-Ling straight after the exams.'

'Sure,' I say happily.

He is cramming his dirty clothes into the laundry bag. 'I miss old Sean. What time did those two guys start today?'

'Later than yesterday. Definitely after nine.'

'A week, they told me. I wonder if that includes Saturday.' Wil's worried face emerges from the neck of a dark blue T-shirt. 'If they don't start till after I leave tomorrow, Cec, would you go up and ask them if they're working Saturday?'

'No trouble.'

Wil is looking with longing at his word processor. 'I'm counting a bit on working here all Saturday and Sunday.'

'So am I, actually.'

'How's Malory?'

I look judicious.

'No magic intervention yet?'

'Not yet.'

'I don't see how one instance would disprove the argument.'

'It would weaken it.'

'It could accommodate one.'

'Also,' I say loudly, 'it would complicate it.'

And I think of the six hundred pages I have still to scrutinise, and suddenly I do get a bit of that pre-examination panic. It gives me a light blow, then departs, or perhaps hovers.

'English is essentially rubbery,' Wil is saying. 'Nothing you do is going to make it neat and natty. But listen, Cec, if Arthur lets you down, you can always fall back on the Knight in the Cart.'

'I decided on Arthur. I've got to stay with him.'

'You don't. That's just pride.'

I won't reply. 'When I did English,' he says, 'all the girls were mad about the Knight in the Cart.'

'Well, it's attractive,' I say, 'all that understated lust.'

'Simply stated, let's say.'

'We're getting into rubber here. Are you hungry?'

'Bloody starving,' says Wil happily.

'So am I. Let's walk over and eat at the Red Rose.'

I feel sorry for Wil when he tries not to look despondent. He puts his hands on his hips and lets his gaze wander. 'It's Thursday, Cec. We could pick something up. Let's go and amble down the aisles.'

But I hate ambling down the aisles with Wil. It makes me feel condemned to what Katie used to call stodgy drudgery. 'And I suppose,' Wil is saying, his eyes having alighted on the laundry bag, 'we had better go to the laundromat.'

'Forget the laundromat,' I say. I spread my arms and take a spin or two round the room, then come back and let my arms shut in a pincer on Wil. 'Oh come on. Let's go to the Red Rose. The walk will do us good. And let's not keep stumbling over this thing about who pays. And maybe I'll go to the laundromat tomorrow, for a little change from the drills.'

He won't look at me. He still looks at the laundry bag.

'Look,' I say, 'I'll take Malory to the laundromat. I can always concentrate in the laundromat.'

He laughs suddenly, and puts an arm across my shoulders. As we go out of the door he says, with exaggerated gloom, 'It sure would be great to have our own laundry.'

The Red Rose is in Glebe. As we walk over in the warm dusk, he tells me about Ed.

'He's got Mum rattled this time. And Dad's not being helpful. Dad's reached the stage of just wanting to thump him.'

'Does Ed thump your father?'

'He tries.'

'I once thumped Mum,' I suddenly say. Myself surprised, I stick my hands in my front pockets. 'And quick as lightning, she thumped me back. It gave me a shock. It was such a change from her usual courtesy. But it isn't one of my bad memories. It seemed so natural.'

'It isn't always a recommendation,' Wil absently murmurs, 'that an action is natural.'

I am angry. In fact, I wouldn't mind thumping *him*. 'Oh,' I say, 'you're too bloody good for me, Wil Meade. You're at a higher evolutionary stage.

You're further removed from the chimpanzee.'

'I know I'm nearly perfect,' says Wil, 'But let's talk about it another time.'

'After the exams,' I say accusingly.

'Right,' he says. 'When there'll be forty-eight hours in every day. I'm sorry, Cec darling. I know how you feel.'

'We'll talk about how I feel,' I say, with reckless bitterness, 'while we're ambling down those rows of grape vines.'

'I've got some news about those grapes,' says Wil.

But we have reached the Red Rose. 'Let's find a table first,' he says.

The Red Rose is Sydneyan with an Italian accent and Asian undertones. It is cheerful and fairly cheap, and is crowded even as early as this. But at the back we see Athol and Rachel, waving hugely. Athol jumps up and hurries to where we're standing at the door.

'Hey, you two, those guys at our table are just leaving. Hang on a tick and we'll eat together.'

Over the round table, we all reach out and touch each other. We grin and say this is marvellous, and this is GREAT. When we tell them about Katie's card, Rachel laughs, affectionate and wry, and Athol says, 'There goes Chaos Katie. I wonder if she keeps this elderly guy waiting.'

'Or if he would catch the Berlin train without her,' says Wil.

'We only had to do it once,' says Rachel. 'Just once.'

Rachel has put on weight, which somehow adds to the impression she gives of being equable and firm. She smiles and says, 'But wasn't it nice the way she didn't resent it? It wouldn't have been the same without Katie.'

'She put us onto some memorable things,' says Wil.

'She certainly made those bells ring,' says Athol, 'but the trouble was, she couldn't tolerate it when they stopped.'

'Or even died down a bit,' says Rachel.

'Hey,' I say, 'What is all this? Are we speaking her epitaph?'

'Yeah,' says Athol, 'when who knows, she might appear in that door right now.'

'With bells ringing,' says Rachel.

We are eating Italian and drinking red wine by the glass. One each. Rachel and Athol are going to stay on Rachel's parents' farm after their exams, and are not looking forward to the distress Rachel's mother displays because they won't set a date for their marriage.

'I know that still goes on,' says Wil.

'It does with them,' says Rachel. 'Not only does Mum want to put us in separate rooms, but she can't keep off the subject, even at breakfast.'

'Especially at breakfast,' says Athol.

'It's even worse when she gets me by myself,' says Rachel. 'Unless Dad comes in and tells her to leave the lass alone, I've got to spring to my feet loudly proclaiming that we'll marry when and if we both feel like it.'

'When else?' I say.

The other three look at me, and we are all silent. Then Rachel says, 'But you're in a different position.'

'Are we talking about the complications caused by my vast fortune?' I ask.

'Yes,' says Athol.

Athol has always been frank, but it strikes me now that he has become self-conscious about it, as if he wants to be known as Honest Athol. He looks at me with this blatant honesty and says, 'Why can't we talk about it?'

'I could tell you why not,' says Wil, but Athol goes virtuously on. 'Investments aren't very attractive these days.'

'It's not invested,' I say. 'It's in a bank. You know those things? Banks?'

'Too bloody well,' says Athol.

'Don't frighten my girl,' says Wil. 'She might bolt.'

'If anything's safe,' says Athol, 'it's property.'

I roll my eyes at the ceiling. 'Like a flat with its own laundry.'

'Yum,' says Rachel.

'Hey, lay off, you two,' says Wil. 'Cec will think it's a conspiracy.'

'Yes,' I say. 'Lay off the big heiress.'

But though they lay off me, they keep on about financial matters. I finish my glass of wine, then put my chin on a hand and pretend to be engrossed in scanning the room. I am in a drinking mood, but none of the others seem even wistful about not having a few more. My eyes catch the eyes of a suntanned guy in a red shirt, but as his look has some kind of intention in it, I emphasise the aimlessness of my own gaze by letting it wander all over. I imagine Katie really appearing in that doorway, running, grinning, and I know that the moment I saw her, I would jump up and wave both arms. I get up muttering about going to the loo, and Rachel gets up too, saying she'll come with me.

'Is this really us?' I say crossly, on our way, 'talking about interest rates and mortgages and things.'

'I agree that it's not intrinsically interesting,' says Rachel, 'but as it affects our lives so much, there's no sense in avoiding it.'

'Such are the claims of the world!' I say, with dramatic boredom.

'You bet,' says Rachel.

The only cubicle is occupied, and at the wash basin a girl is leaning towards the mirror engrossedly watching her mouth as she applies lipstick with a small brush. Rachel turns her back to me, flips up her skirt, and shows me her knickers. They are skin-tight black lace, with a purple and gold butterfly on each buttock. 'Very agricultural,' I say. The girl retracts her head to assess her work. When she goes out, Rachel says, 'Athol and I believe that the current narcissism had its origin in Japan.'

'No doubt,' I say sourly, 'during Japan's financial supremacy.'

'I hope you don't think you're being ironical,' says Rachel.

After the cubicle is free, and Rachel and I have peed, we stand at the wash basin and each talk into the other's face in the mirror as we wash our hands and brush our hair.

'Now that Athol's put his foot in it,' says Rachel, 'I'm going to put mine in too. About that money, just tell me one thing.'

'What is it?' I say, careful but not surly.

'I often wonder whether your mother added that marriage condition on impulse, you know, in a codicil.'

'No,' I say absently, leaning forward and looking into my own eyes. 'It was in the body of the will, made five or six weeks before she died.'

Rachel has taken her eye drops from her bag, and now she takes off her specs and gives them to me to hold. 'But she made it after she knew?'

'Oh, for sure.'

'Well,' says Rachel, 'you can imagine her state of mind.'

'But I can't,' I say. 'That's exactly what I can't do.'

Rachel's head drops forward, and she looks at me with one eye suffused. 'Cec, don't get excited.'

'And exactly what I keep trying to do.'

'Cec, a cliche. Spoken without thinking. I'm sorry.'

She tilts her head back again. 'All I was getting round to suggesting,' she says, from that distance, 'was that if it would cost so much to challenge that clause, just wait till Wil's qualified, and he can do it, and he would be sure to win, and you could get married without feeling pressured.'

'And if he didn't?' I ask.

'You'd have cleared the decks. Has anyone thought of that?'

'Everyone,' I am pleased to say.

'All of it?' she asks, blinking like mad.

'Different words, same song.'

'Then why not do it?'

I am giving her back her specs. 'Because,' I say, 'I would feel too low, having a last posthumous quarrel with my mother.'

'I see-e.' Rachel puts on her specs and looks at me closely. 'And I suppose, especially if you won?'

'Now that you mention it.'

'I see-e.'

'It's only,' she says, as we go out, 'that Wil's such a marvellous guy.'

I am so used to hearing this that I automatically agree as I weave after her through the tables. But really, I am wondering why, after puzzling for so long about my instinctive recoil from that legal challenge, I should speak out the answer, without thinking at all, while standing at the wash basin giving Rachel back her specs. It feels like some kind of progress. I add it to the list of things I won't tell Wil. Near our table, Rachel slows down to say, 'Don't look now, but there's a gorgeous guy over to the right fancies you. I noticed him before. Red shirt. Great tan.'

'I refuse to look,' I say, 'because of Saint Wil.'

Rachel giggles. 'I bet those two are still talking about money.'

But Wil and Athol are talking about fibre optics.

'The most facile conclusion,' Athol is saying, 'is that it will put an end to the isolation out there.'

'It must help,' says Wil.

'Not if the people out there can't bloody afford it,' says Athol. 'That technology costs. In those remote areas most of them haven't got Buckley's chance.'

Rachel sits down and says with social animation, 'I'm never quite sure who this Buckley is.'

'He was a convict,' says Wil, 'who escaped, from Hobart, I think, and set out to walk to China.'

We all laugh happily at poor Buckley. In the lingering surprise of my discovery, I am feeling light-hearted. 'My grandmother,' I say, 'traced her ancestors in the UK. She told everyone about the convict, but kept quiet about the scullery maid.'

'And told everyone she was keeping quiet about her,' says Wil.

We all laugh at Gran. We divvy up the bill. Rachel and Athol give me their share, and I pay as we pass the cash register at the door. Outside we stand in facing pairs, idly resisting farewells, trying to set a date for another meeting. Feeling happy under Wil's arm, and facing friends, I move in a tiny, almost stationary shuffle. Rain begins to fall, scarcely more than a mist. 'It will be good for the crops,' I say, and while Rachel contracts her face at this townie joke, Athol proposes a meeting in early December.

'No good,' I say. 'We'll be picking grapes.'

And Christmas, we all agree, is hopelessly shredded. It will have to be January. So we part, waving backwards through the rain and calling, 'January,' and, 'We'll ring.'

'We ought to have said who will ring who,' I complain to Wil.

'You can't nail everything down.'

In Wigram Road, I take his arm. He seems displeased with me, though pretending not to be. I wonder if it is about my townie joke, but decide not to try to nail it down. So I start babbling, which I sometimes do in nervous moments.

'Wasn't it great seeing them? It's been months. And don't you love rain like this? It makes Wigram Road look so beautiful. I mean it shrouds its usually rather excessive beauty.'

'Listen, Cec,' says Wil, in an intentional way.

'Listen, Cec,' I mock, sing-song.

'About that grape-picking.'

'About that grape-picking?'

'They're taking only experienced pickers this year.'

'Well, didn't I pick grapes on Crete?'

'For ten days.'

'Oh, I see. Whereas you?'

'Yes, Cec, I'm classed as a professional. I picked for these people for three seasons when they were at Mudgee.'

I stop and face him. But he says, 'Oh, come on, Cec love, it's raining.' And this time he puts an arm across my shoulders and propels us forward.

'You mean,' I say, 'you're going alone.'

'No alternative, Cec.'

'Then what will I do?'

'Do?' In the light rain, in the darkness, I see his face turned towards me. 'Coopers will give you work. December? Lots of casuals needed? Office parties? Won't they?'

I dismiss Coopers with a hand. I know they will give me work. I am a good waitress, being fast, strong, and deft. 'That's not what I mean,' I say.

'Then what do you mean, Cec?'

But now I am ashamed of my spontaneous self-betrayal. His critical tone makes my longing for his uninterrupted company seem like a weak dependence. 'Why didn't you tell me before?' I mutter. 'Why did you let me tell people about it?'

'I know. Sorry about that. But I only heard it myself today. Mum told me. I did have a few doubts, though, Cec. That's partly why I rang Mum. That and to check on young Ed. Things have changed, see? since we first planned it. Unemployment in those western towns means they can get pickers galore. And Mum was a bit concerned about another thing, Cec. Have you ever been out west?'

'I know what you're going to say, but yes, I have, to Broken Hill. And yes, it was on a school excursion.'

'In winter?'

'Now you're going to tell me about the heat.'

'You've no conception of it, darling. Look, I blame myself. It was stupid and unimaginative of me, making those plans.'

I say in a low voice, 'You don't have to go either.'

'Yes, I do,' says Wil.

'Coopers might take you too.'

'I like these people,' says Wil, 'and I like what they're doing. This early picking is for the new Asian export market.'

'Oh. Well, I can't argue with anything as splendid

and patriotic as that, can I?'

'Not really, Cec,' says Wil. 'But listen, love, you want to see Athol and Rachel when they come back from the farm. Right, you'll be in Sydney, so get in touch.'

'We've always seen them together,' I say feebly.

'Things change, Cec.'

'And I can't help thinking,' I say, 'that they can't want to see us as much as all that, or else they would have rung when they decided to come over this way tonight.'

'They did. And they rang Sean and Chun-Ling too.'

'Oh, aren't they marvellous,' I say. 'Aren't they bloody marvels.'

Wil laughs a bit and tightens his grip on my shoulders. 'Those two were out, and our line was engaged.'

'Oh,' I say, 'me and Gene.'

'I guess so,' says Wil. 'let's get a move-on, Cec. I'm not mad about getting wet.'

I try to hang back. I am arrested by the effect of my own words, Me and Gene. But Wil, without exactly propelling me, makes me hurry. Wil is good at silent persuasion. Mum, when she remarked on his pleasantly confident manner towards me, said it probably came from being the eldest child. Sometimes I resist Wil's assumption of authority, but tonight I am distracted by the sorrow that struck me as I spoke those two words, Me and Gene. By fast stages I retrieve the detail of our childhood dream of living together, just us two, me and Gene, in rich simplicity, nourishing ourselves with love and justice, with books and music, with simple food and natural beauty. Water featured in our intention, perhaps a pond. Yes, we had been reading Mum's copy of *Walden*. Now, as those old images and that old mood were exposed, and lifted out of me, I felt as if some lighted space inside me had gone dark. It was another unbelievable absence, and it made me want to stop under a tree and cry out that this time last year I had so much, and ask why I have been left with so little. But I can't do this, not to Wil, not only because it would be insulting, but because it would make me see myself, reflected in the mirror of Wil's principles, as disgracefully self-indulgent in view of the various deprivations around me, to say nothing of the sorrow, terror, famine, and the clash of ignorant armies in the terrible world outside. Wil wants to live his life in full consciousness of that world, he genuinely does, and so would I, perhaps, but whatever I do, my concerns remain narrow, and I often forget all about it.

If I had hung back, and given my howl of woe about my losses, Wil would not have reproached me. He is never harsh. He might even have comforted me. But I would still see that reflection of myself, and worse, would have shown it to him. So I don't howl out my grief, but trudge along at Wil's side, a female chimpanzee, passing alone through the melancholy primeval forest. Wil is silent, too, until we come to our street door, and then he looks up and says reflectively, 'I don't think many renovators work Saturday, especially during the cricket.'

While we are taking off our damp clothes, the heat accumulated in the shut-up flat, and the clamminess of our skins, make us fall almost automatically into sexual positions. We fall onto the bed. It is fast. It is purposeful. It is undeflected by the ringing phone. But the vertiginous moments, the absence from myself, don't leave as residue their usual lovely sensuous mood, perhaps because those three rings, happening at our peak, had wrenched from us a single gasp of laughter.

So we looked close into each other's eyes and kissed, quick, sharp, repeatedly, in thanks perhaps, then got up and washed, and each in turn, cleaned our teeth, and then went together to bed. Wil wondered who that was on the phone, and I said that whoever it was, they could ring again in the morning. He said he hoped it wasn't his mother about young Ed, and I said in a rough wifely manner, 'To hell with young Ed. Let's go to sleep.'

I take myself by surprise when I talk like that. It forecasts the kind of married settlement that Katie and I used to say was the dread and horror of our lives.

Wil goes into a heavy sleep, lying as still as an overturned stone column. There is something uncanny about the decorousness of Wil's sleep. He used to sleep like that even on trains. 'I think he's dead,' Katie would say, but the others said it was a great gift, being able to sleep like that. Yeah yeah.

I settle beside him like an architecturally inferior column, but I don't shut my eyes. In the privacy of lone wakefulness, I return to thoughts of Eugene,

trying to discover why the Me and Gene ideal persisted, not quite forgotten but not acknowledged,
for so long. Possibly because, after it was knocked out
of us by our gain in worldly knowledge, we never
spoke of it. Either in sorrow at our loss, or, more
likely, in adolescent shame at our naivety, our
agreement on silence was tacit, and so, I theorise in
the dark, it was like those countries we never reach,
and its ideal essence remained intact.

The phone rings again, but as I roll over reaching
out an arm, it stops. I swing out my legs and sit on the
edge of the bed. I turn on the little lamp, look at
the phone, and say Ah-ha to myself. Bursts of two or
three rings are known to be typical of Gran. First of
all, Aunt Gail says, Gran calculates what time it is in
Sydney, then suddenly loses confidence in her cal-
culations, and hangs up until she can consult some
chart, or some person, and try again. I sympathise
because, when I used to ring her, soon after I came
back, I was a bit like that myself. But now it seems
indisputable that the time in London would be
half-past twelve and that it would be better for me to
ring Gran than to be kept awake in expectation of
more of those nervous bursts.

Besides, Gran is not often barricaded by busy-
ness, and though the cost of international calls is
sometimes a substitute for that barricade, at other
times she will say, 'Hang the expense. Throw the
cat a goldfish,' which is one of her twenties or thirties
sayings. And if this happens, we might say something interesting to each other, for a change.

So I tip the lampshade away from Wil, consult

the list taped to the wall, and tap out Gran's number. She answers after two rings. 'Hello, Gran,' I say, in a bright surprised childish voice.

'It's Cecily.' Gran sounds incredulous. 'Well! Cec!'

'Gran, did you ring just then?'

She says, deeply mystified, 'No-o.'

And I am mystified too, mystified all over again by those inaudible transmissions of truth by telephone. I don't mean the kind caused by people trusting in their invisibility and so not guarding their voices, but this kind, the mysterious kind, that make me wonder if those orbiting satellites have escaped their origins and now partake of the miraculous. Yes (I want to believe) they do. And it seems to me too that the miracle is not diminished, but compounded, by the great distance, so that Gran's shame-faced deceit is as evident as if she was an actor playing it out on a screen. I laugh in delight, and she laughs in response, rather uncertainly, before I tell her what she wants to know.

'It's eleven-thirty p.m. here.'

'Yes, as if I would ring at this hour.' Her scoffing tone is for those who would. 'Now you hang up, dear, like you used to do, and I'll ring you back.'

I hang up, pleased with this game that has come my way. Because of Mum's famous embargo, Gran is the only person I have ever spoken to on an international line at my own instigation, and on those earlier occasions I was too distraught, and too frustrated by her imperturbability, and her failure to answer my questions, to enjoy the miraculous element, or even to notice if it differed from the local or national version.

I pick up the phone as soon as it rings. 'This is quite a coincidence, Cec,' says Gran, 'because I had in mind to ring you tomorrow, to wish you and Wil all the best for your exams.'

'Thank you, Gran.'

'You can be over-confident, you know.'

'Ha,' I say, 'I know who you've been talking to.'

'Nick rings every week, that's true,'

'I meant Aunt Gail.'

'Gail did come on for a while.'

'I've done a lot of work during the year, Gran, and I'm still doing a bit.'

'Only a bit, Cec?'

'Enough.'

'Oh well,' says Gran, who doesn't really give a damn about exams. 'And I'm sure,' she adds with relief, 'that Wil's a good influence.'

'Absolutely,' I say. 'Marvellous.'

It doesn't matter at all what words I use. My awed attention is all for those two small voices isolated in that huge alert space. And now, when I hear, in Gran's flat, a door shutting, I call out, 'And at last I can talk to Uncle Ugo.'

'Cec dear, I'm sorry, no. It's funny the way you always miss Ugo.'

'I heard a door.'

'The door. That was Toby.'

'Toby?'

'A sort of friend of Ugo's, who was in a bit of a spot. I've given them the big room, the one you called the ballroom, and I'm in the other one, that's why you could hear the door. It's easier for me in many ways, and it won't be for long.'

Gran lives in an old apartment block in St John's Wood. To the left of her door is a good-sized bedroom, then the kitchen, then the bathroom, then a big living room, and then the huge bedroom I called her ballroom. This amused her very much, and she stood in the doorway, and folded her hands, and said, 'Well, I like a swanky bedroom.'

'It was my own suggestion,' she is saying now, 'the changeover. Though to tell you the truth,' and now a sullenness reaches me, 'to tell you the truth, Toby's no great favourite of mine.'

'Is he a musician?'

'Oh my goodness, no. What can you be thinking of? Toby's a painter.'

Gran pronounces the word painter with deep, impossible respect. 'Oh and Cec, incidentally, don't mention Toby to your Uncle Nick. He would tell me to take a stand, though as I said, the changeover was my own suggestion, and it's just till Toby finds something.'

It is easy, on the stretch of my attention, to imagine I hear Mum's voice, a third across the spaces, singing that doting always has a victim. But Gran is saying, with a kind of grinding belligerence, that it's not that she's afraid of Toby, and that nobody should run away with that idea, and then I, not knowing how to respond, say on impulse, 'Describe him.'

My grandmother gives a little shriek. 'Describe Toby?'

'Go on,' I say, not quite bullying, 'describe him.'

'All right.' And my grandmother, Eleanor Campbell Ambrussi, prepares to match my boldness. 'I will, then. Hang the expense. Throw the cat a goldfish.' She waits for me to laugh, and when I do, she laughs herself, then goes eagerly on. 'Well now, Toby. Let me see. Toby. He's twenty-eight. He says he's twenty-eight. And he's one of those pale-skinned boys with dirty-looking golden hair. Not real dirt of course. And not grey. Certainly not. How could that be? Let's say dusty gold. How does that sound? And real round loopy curls. And smiles a lot. And on the fat side.'

'He sounds like the cupid type,' I say.

'So he might have been,' she says, 'once.'

'What does he paint?'

'Nothing that I can decipher. It's funny, there's that little fair fat chap, and he just paints the gloomiest biggest blackest things you ever saw.'

How clearly I see those dark objects against the swags of white frilled muslin in Gran's huge bedroom. I say helplessly, 'Uncle Ugo must love him.'

There is a marvellously eloquent silence. Then Gran says primly, 'Toby's had a very hard life.'

But I am bold again. 'Does he put his feet up on your pink velvet sofa?'

Gran bursts into a relieved laugh. 'Just let him try!'

'You would take a stand?'

'You bet I would,' cries Eleanor Ambrussi.

I send a laugh off into space. 'This is lovely, Gran.'

'It's one of those wonderful lines you get. And it's nice to have a talk. I was feeling the need. And,' she adds defensively, 'you're grown-up now.'

'I am supposed to be,' I say.

'But not really? Is that about the size of it?'

I am startled by this change to a rough tone. I lose the illusion of the miraculous, or perhaps some actual variation in the sound waves deprives me of it. I might now be sitting opposite Gran's pink velvet sofa, or in the window-seat of the flat at Kirribilli she lived in for a while after Granddad died. I say meekly, 'What makes you think I'm not grown-up, Gran?'

'Well, have you condescended to see your father yet?'

'Aunt Gail,' I say, 'is like a sheep dog who thinks I'm a sheep.'

'It's not your aunt at all.' She retreats, is evasive again. 'It's been on my mind since your father moved to Sydney.'

'Which was three years ago,' I say, with deadly calm.

'And don't tell me in all that time you haven't run into him?'

I start to say, with my best tolerant bewilder-ment, that Sydney is a big city, but she interrupts.

'I mean, you would think, seeing he's a univer-sity professor and you're a student.'

'He might be a professor now, Gran,' I say. 'He was a lecturer in modern history last time I heard of him. And we're not in the same university. And unless you have friends in the other three universities, you don't know much of what goes on in them.'

Sometimes Gran boasts that anything to do with tertiary education is double-dutch to her, and sometimes she pretends to know all about it. 'Well,' she now says, with a sort of unctuous indignation, 'of course you wouldn't. Four universities. It would be like expecting to know everybody in a town. Worse, because they're probably spread out all over the place, like everything there nowadays. That's what I couldn't stand, everything spread out. But they say the education is good, and if there's one thing I'm glad of, Cec, it's that you're getting the benefit of some of your grandfather's money.'

I murmur something polite. Then there is a silence. I feel the weight of it, a weight transmitted into her next words. 'If it had been up to me alone, I would have done more.'

And before I can divert her, she goes on. 'For Chris. Helped her more. It was your grandfather who wouldn't. He let her have the use of the house, and willed her half of it, then said No More. And not all my entreaties.'

Gran had told me this in London, though not in this grinding tone. 'He took a stand,' I say gaily.

'You can laugh if you like,' says Gran, and goes on before I can deny it. 'Laugh if you like, but after your grandfather passed on, and I offered help off my own bat, she refused point-blank.'

'But she didn't. You've forgotten,' I tell her, 'you paid for my journey.'

'Oh, for you she accepted. Anything precisely and specifically for you. But for herself, or for general expenses, no thank you.'

I am trying to interrupt. I want to remind her that Mum's frugality was almost a philosophical stand. But Gran is saying, 'And if I tried to insist, she would just give me one of those kind smiles of hers, and not say one more word.'

I am silenced by the kind smile. 'And the upshot of it was,' says Gran, 'I felt snubbed.'

I start to say I am sure she didn't mean, etc., but in fact I am not sure, and anyway, Gran is off again.

'Oh, I know there was also my so-called favouritism for Ugo. I am well aware of that. But Chris knew just as well as I did that I felt responsible for Ugo. Even for the asthma, according to some medical opinion. The fact is, he should never have been sent to a GPS school. And that was my doing. Your grandfather was against it. It was me who talked him round. And do you know why? Snobbery. Snobbery pure and simple. We had made the money by then, and the boys had to have the best. That was my thinking.'

'Uncle Nick –' I say.

'Played football,' interrupts my grandmother, triumphant and flat. 'Played football, and was bigger. You could get away with being a half-Eye-tie if you were big, and made the footy team.'

I begin to ask why she didn't take Ugo away from the school, but again she interrupts. 'And Nick was also,' she says with dignity, 'different in his make-up. Ugo had his sweet nature and his kindness even then, and it was the very boys who were nastiest to him he adored the most, and wouldn't be parted from.'

And when I start to speak again, she forestalls me again. 'Oh yes, I know you'll say all that's changed. I know very well it's different these days. But it was a racist old place in those days, your wonderful Australia.'

While she goes on about this, including what it was like for her to be married to an Eye-tie, or Dago, as they were called in those days, and how her mother and brother never spoke to her again, I am trying to assemble the words to tell her that racism is a relic of our descent from the tribally aggressive chimpanzee, and that having evolved so far, we will keep on, though, unfortunately, there will be some unevenness, even some regression, and so on. But now my grandmother is saying, 'And I'm willing to bet odds-on that underneath all this great Aussie multi-racial hoo-hah, things haven't really changed all that much, even if your Uncle Nick did tell me this morning, without turning a hair, that Gene has got himself a Chinese girlfriend.'

I am shocked. My lies go round the world. It takes me a second or two to remember that it is no longer a lie, but has evolved, with slight variations, into reality.

'Well, just let us wait,' Gran is saying, 'let us wait six months, say, and see how they're getting on then with Miss Ching-a-Ling.'

'That's not her name,' I say, urgently enough to penetrate Gran's absorption.

'I beg your pardon, Cec,' she says. 'That is her name. Here it is on my phone pad. Miss Ching-a-

Ling. I wrote it like that as a sort of a joke, then crossed out the a.'

'Gran,' I say, 'there's been some confusion. I was talking to Gene this evening. He told me her name is Susan Wu.'

'That's funny then.'

'Susan Wu,' I repeat.

'Are you sure?'

'Gran, Gene would know.'

'Well, if that's what he told you. Susan Wu. Susie Wu. That sounds rather sweet. Oh, I'm not saying it won't work. It's not for us to predict. But I'll tell you one thing, Cec. Miss Susie, or Miss Ching-a-Ling or whatever, had better be chic, or those twins will give her curry.'

As I laugh, and she laughs, the sound waves vary again, or the mystery re-asserts itself, and before I can tell her about Susan Wu's father's fruit and veg, she says the cat's had enough of the goldfish, and that she is sorry I seem fated to miss Ugo, who is in Lucca at present, in fact, staying with his cousin Carla.

This makes me forget Susan Wu. I lean into the phone and say angrily, 'He likes Carla?'

'They're great mates.'

'Carla,' I say, 'let her mother scream at me.'

'Didn't I warn you about Etta?' Gran calls out, pleased.

'Carla didn't even try to stop her.'

'Ah, but you see, Cec, Etta holds the purse strings.'

There is a sort of wisdom and settlement in Gran's voice as she tells me this. Then I hear her saying Good-bye again, and Best Wishes again, and I rouse myself to say faintly:

'Good-bye, Gran. And thank you.'

Wil has not moved.

I sit on the edge of the bed and press my hands between my knees to stop myself from shaking him awake to tell him about the purse strings. He knows the rest already. I had to tell someone, and he was the only one home in our clean grim old pensione when I came back from my visit. And he made me come straight out again, saying that a walk on the ramparts would make me feel better, and improve my coherence.

I get up from the bed and go softly to our work table and tilt the light towards me. From the thin white layer of the airmail pads I extract the bottom one. I hadn't been keeping them for long then, and hadn't got into all those esoteric space-saving devices, so the entry is easy to read. I wrote it on the train out of Lucca. This is it.

I didn't like that town from the start. It felt sinister to me, and on the hot drizzly day we walked in, the little alleys smelled of rats. I rang Mum's old friend, my second cousin Carla, and was put off by her formality. But then suddenly she changed to English, and said Yes, do come. Come for coffee, she said, and named a time two days ahead. She asked if I knew the way, and I said Yes, thank you, I had a map.

The rain stopped, and we found a little shop where we could buy cheap adventurous food, a bit of this and that and that, so that we could make up picnics and spend the siesta eating and resting in the shade of the wonderful green and golden trees on the broad ramparts. It was early autumn. On one particular day I was so happy there, lying half-asleep in the luscious grass, that for about three minutes I even went into one of my covetous fantasies.

But I still couldn't come to terms with what those roseate walls enclosed. I shrank from the gruesome religious relics, and from the bright sardonic eyes of bystanders in doorways watching the evening passagiata. There was no outdoor eating, and in a cheap trattoria at night I saw wives colouring the water in their glasses with a splash of their husband's wine. What held me uncomplainingly there was my appointment with Carla, and the opinion of the others that it was the ideal place to rest up and poke around in. Katie liked even the religious relics. 'Dreadful things have happened here,' she said with satisfaction.

On the third day, I put on clean jeans, and a fresh white shirt, and changed my runners for the supple plaited leather shoes I had bought in Florence. In the shadow of one of the newer gates, I unfolded my map, then trotted out like a good little girl to visit my Ambrussi kin.

I wasn't nervous. Why should I be? If they didn't like me, too bad. I would just trot off again, and re-join my friends, and in two days, or three, we would leave that town forever.

After all the crumbly stuff inside the walls, I

quite liked the big new angular innocent-looking house. 'Arrivo,' I whispered to myself. Set in tiles beside the front door, a round pond held artificial water lilies. A squat young maid let me in. In the hall, above gilded furniture, hung a calmly crucified Christ in pastels and gold. I trotted happily enough after the maid into the open door of a small sitting room, where Carla rose from a chair to greet me.

She was a thin fiftyish woman, and wore a pleated tartan skirt, a grey silk shirt, and a lot of new-looking gold jewellery. When we had touched hands, she sat down again, and tilted her head at the same angle as the madonna in the oval frame behind her chair.

She asked if I spoke Italian, and when I said, with the usual deprecating shrug, Yes, she suggested that all the same, we should speak English. I said Of course, and she launched into polite questions about my journey, and then about my travelling companions and my present accommodation. I heard in her intonation and phrasing the influence of her teacher, my mother, and when I leaned forward, and laughed as I told her so, she smiled, then looked aside, tapped one cheek, and said in a different tone, petulant or playfully injured, that she had a toothache, and must go to her dentist within the hour.

Confused, I was about to stand up and say that since she had an appointment, and so on, but just then the maid brought me coffee in a cup, and one cake on a plate. Carla took nothing, but because she tapped her cheek in explanation, I stayed. While I drank the coffee, she told me about her five children, the youngest, Giancarlo, my own age, and then about her husband's opinion of the careers chosen by those children. All this she said with the same girlish petulance, or perhaps playful injury, in which she had spoken of her toothache. It occurred to me that I had often heard that same tone, lately, in the speech of well-dressed Italian matrons, and a curiosity about it diverted me from my intention to leave. I was listening to it attentively, and wondering if it would be rude to ask her questions about it, when an old woman flung (yes, *flung*) open the door, and walked up to my chair.

Carla murmured something, perhaps Mama, while her Mama, my great-aunt Antonietta, stood looking down at me, breathing hoarsely. She was shinily and elaborately dressed in black, and her ankles, thinned to the bone, looked in their black stockings as if they would break under her great ungainly weight.

I couldn't believe that it was I – *me* – who was being looked at with such malevolence. It paralysed me. It arrested me in the act of rising. And then, after a few more hoarse breaths, she opened up on me.

And how could I believe this, either? I didn't understand all her swift Italian, but I clearly understood that I was being called the bastard daughter of a whore to whom they had once, in their trust and innocence, their Christian charity, given shelter, and that I, I myself, was also a shameless Australian whore, who had been seen, yes, seen by her own servants, roaming the town and countryside with a band of riff-raff.

And in all this, too, was a variation of that petulance, not at all playful now, but sunk into deep and thrilling injury. Shame was mentioned, also corruption, also disgrace to a family much honoured, and which had once had a palazzo within those walls (to which she was indignantly pointing, though without taking her gaze from my face). Those walls, she repeated, now polluted by those who had abandoned the church of the true God.

And so on.

By now I had got over my first state of shocked disbelief, and had come to the conclusion that this woman was insane, and could not be held responsible. With difficulty, I turned my head away from her glistening black bulk and looked questioningly at Carla.

Carla was sitting with her head turned aside and one hand raised to her mouth not quite hiding a slight smile.

I jumped to my feet. I felt the blood rush to my face as I met my great-aunt's eyes. She was now speaking, in her furiously injured tone, of my grandfather, her own brother, the apostate, from whom all this evil had sprung. Her faded black eyes did not flinch from mine, but glittered in steady triumph, and her vibrant voice did not once falter. To get out I had actually to push against her body, and I can't forget the smell of it, of dry cleaning, of hair spray, of old talcumed flesh.

Carla had not moved. The vehement voice was punching me towards the door. Her own brother, my grandfather. Shame, Shame, the deep-throated 'Vergogna!' As I ran down the hall I saw in my side vision, hovering, the young maid, with a taller woman behind her, their slyly angled bodies, their passive pleasure.

Out of the door, leaping past the water lilies, as out of a pausing car in the street leapt a young man, laughing, extending both hands. 'The Australian cousin. I am Giancarlo.' I didn't stop moving as I told him, with the full force of the spiteful ferocious Italian Katie and Rachel and I had practised in Rome, to leave me alone.

This did me good. The vengeful blood coursing through me stopped me from shaking. But it didn't stop me from walking in the wrong direction. I knew it was wrong, but to be seen, even by myself, to hesitate, to have made a mistake, was intolerable. And in that broad clean street I saw nowhere to hide, no tree, no bus shelter, no niche in a wall. So, sniffing up my tears, banging down my heels, and tossing my head, I walked to the next corner, and once around it, stopped, leaned against a new yellow wall, and bent my head over my map.

I bowed my head more deeply as a big tourist bus sped past, returning from the legendary, beloved countryside.

Forty minutes later, I was walking on the ramparts with Wil, his arm tight around my shoulders. Though it was not siesta, we saw nobody on the ramparts except two strolling, smiling German tourists, and as I finished my story, a local couple fucking in one of the ditches.

'It's a small provincial town, after all,' said Wil. 'Tourism gives it a deceptive screen. Your great-aunt's maid's sister probably vacuums our rooms.'

'You're always looking for excuses for people,' I said. 'You're so bloody tolerant. I suppose you think I ought to have been nice to bloody Giancarlo?'

'Not on your life,' said Wil. 'If people believe in paying for the sins of their fathers, let them pay a bit themselves.'

This sounded vindictive enough to console me. 'I want to leave here tomorrow,' I said.

'Okay with me. We'll put it to the others.'

'I hated it here from the start. I told them that, didn't I?'

'Tell them again, then.'

'Not about what she said. I've told you. That's enough. I can't bear to tell them.'

'Not even Katie?'

'Not even Katie. The humiliation, you see? You understand?'

Wil didn't understand, and neither did I, quite, unless my confrontation with my great-aunt was a sort of dramatic summation of a hundred little hints, a hundred little changes in atmosphere, in an infancy otherwise obscured. Perhaps, even, my great-aunt's eyes reminded me of eyes looking down at me from above the red waistcoat of my grandfather. If I saw his waistcoat, I must have seen his face, mustn't I? So why is the one remembered, I would like to know, and the other blotted out? But this is only surmise, of course.

The entry ends there, but the incident didn't, not quite. Though I couldn't bear to tell the others about my humiliation, I did intend to tell my mother. I hid from Wil my seething intention to write to her that night, to tell her about all the furious words, about Carla's half-hidden smile, everything. 'And you,' I intended to write, 'encouraged me to visit them.'

The main reason I didn't write that letter was because, as Wil and I were descending into the city, there popped up, from the memory of that diatribe punching me towards the door, the words 'common vendor of fruit'. I halted Wil. I faced him. 'Hey,' I said, and laughed, and gave him a backward flip on the chest. 'Do you know what? Even the fruit and veg copped a serve.'

Wil made big eyes. 'Not the fruit and veg,' he said, hushed.

'Yes,' I said happily, 'which have been good to us.'

So when I wrote to Mum that night, I kept it jokey, and let the fruit and veg star. 'You can imagine,' I wrote, 'my shock and horror.'

Another reason I spared her was time. The jokiness was also in the interest of brevity. We were packing. I told the others hardly anything about my visit. Only about the water lilies, the nicely painted cruci-fixion, and the one cup of coffee and one cake on a plate. But I expressed again my revulsion for the city, reminded them that I had hated it from the start, and begged them to let us move on next morning.

Katie supported me. She said my revulsion probably had its origins in ancestral memory, and that an Ambrussi, or, over the centuries, quite a number of them, had been put to death in horrible ways within these walls. I remember how Sean laughed at her description of the horrible ways. That was before he decided she was a sensationalist, but still thought she was a lovely sexy original girl.

I don't remember where we were when I got Mum's reply to my letter. It was even briefer than mine.

Oh dear, poor old Aunt Etta. She was always a zealot, and they do tend to go mad. So that part wasn't surprising. But the water lilies amazed me.

I have to move all the books to put the airmail pad back in its place. And after I've done that, I run the palm of my hand along the side to make it indistinguishable from the rest. Very neat. I suppose Mum knew about her Aunt Etta holding the purse strings, and if I had told the whole thing, about all the words, and that theatrically furtive little smile of Carla's, she would have made the same excuse for Carla as Gran did tonight.

'Ah, but you see, Cec, Etta holds the purse strings.'

But in a different tone.

Yes, sitting at our work table in the silence, I can hear her.

I turn off the table light, creep back across the room, and pick up my watch from beside the phone. Twenty-five to one. Wil rolls over onto his side, and his breathing changes, becomes audible. I switch off the bedside light, get into bed, haul up my legs, roll over, and curl into his back. I know he won't wake, and nor he does. He gives one longish subterranean heave, but he doesn't wake.

Dislodged by the heave, I lie on my back, lightly shut my eyes, pull down my suspended list of things I won't tell him, and add to it the purse strings that twitched Carla's lips.

Then I let the list rise again. Suspending it is not as good as being able to tell it, but it does give me a drowsy little satisfaction that I wonder at.

FRIDAY

IN THE MORNING, I FEEL obliged to detach a few of Gran's words from the list.

'Gran rang after you went to sleep last night. She wanted to wish us both all the best for the exams.'

'Thank you,' says Wil. 'I've often wondered if you could ask her, some time, if the Mafia was active in the wholesale markets during your grandfather's time there.'

'She would have to make the opportunity herself.'

'Of course,' says Wil, slightly offended.

He and I are estranged this morning. It is as if we simultaneously have an instinct to remove ourselves for a while. This happens every now and again, for no discernible reason. On these occasions, I have to say, we remind me slightly of those stiff-legged circling dogs. When Wil says good-bye he sounds apologetic about reminding me to see Scotty and Clark.

Scotty and Clark don't arrive till about ten. By the time I hear their truck stop outside, I have already scrutinised more than one hundred pages, mostly of Isolde the Fair, using the edge of a card to run down under each line and stopping whenever I see the word King, or king, or Arthur.

I give Scotty and Clark time to get upstairs, then follow them. Wil would know which was Scotty and which was Clark, but I don't. I stand in the doorway as they raise their heads and look at me cautiously.

'Will there be much drilling today?'

They confer with their eyes. 'Not much,' says one.

'Will it be in the morning or the afternoon?'

They confer again. 'Hard to say,' says the other.

'And what about tomorrow?'

'What, Saturday?' They come to life. They speak together. 'Nothing. No noise. No work. No way!'

I go back to Isolde the Fair. But not to be taken by surprise, I plug my ears and put on the headset before going on with my scanning. I am sorry about having to broach with a piece of card and a mechanical mind this tale that less than three years ago could send me into whirls of romantic fantasy. Also, in this dense text, there are kings other than Arthur, notably the baleful Mark, and Arthur himself is often named but does not appear, so the process is slow and witless, and after a while my mind begins its darting. I am like one of those mothers you see with a little kid near a swimming pool. I have to keep grabbing it and bringing it back. It races towards Uncle Ugo, then towards Susan Wu, then stares into Gran's ballroom, then at Mum coming with one arm outstretched to the train, then wants to stagger off to the laundromat. When the drilling starts, muffled by my devices, it actually improves my concentration. It steadies or stuns the darter.

When Mum was tired, she would put on a disc of Bach toccatas before going back to her word processor. 'A wicked misuse, no doubt,' she would say, 'but it steadies me.'

(Straight-backed on her chair, a long arm reaching across and picking up a sheet of paper. Holding it at arm's length with a thumb and index finger gripping the page at mid-top. Sometimes a nod, sometimes a burst of laughter.)

I begin to be grimly pleased by my progress down the pages. I find no magic intervention in Arthur's fate, though magic is freely employed elsewhere. I finish Isolde and race through Lamerok de Galys, then get up and make coffee. I drink it standing, then remove my muffling gear, put Malory and two apples into my bag, grab the bag of laundry, and run out, banging the door.

There is a letter for Wil in the box. Thick, grimy, the envelope twisted by careless pasting. From Ed. I put it in my bag. I warn myself against losing it till after the exams. I am not Wil's keeper.

It is true that I can always concentrate in the laundromat. The whirring and soft thudding is one of the ideal underlying distractions, and the darter is absorbed by a duty to note the cycle of the machine.

The only other users are two guys, both young, both reading. As I sit down after filling the machine, the nearer one looks up from his book. I feel his look on my face, and suppose he wants to talk. If I didn't love talking myself, I wouldn't mind this, but I have to be stern to guard against my own weakness.

On top of a pile of magazines on a low table, a newspaper is folded open at one of those interviews with students who have exams looming, with photos and fears and methods of study and so on. The nearer guy gets up and slides it under a magazine, and the other one gives an appreciative Huh! as the nearer one returns to his seat. I feel his eyes on my face again, but I don't go Huh! or even shift my eyes from the page, though I see in my side vision, as he sits down, that he has a great suntan. He is wearing shorts and a red shirt, and as he is one of those people with naturally attractive flesh, and could even be the one Rachel said fancied me in the Red Rose, I have an added inducement to keep my eyes on Malory.

I eat the apples while scrutinising La Cote Mal Tayle, and have started on Tristam's Madness and Exile when the machine stops, and I get up to transfer the load to a dryer before going on.

I read slowly now. I know that here, in North Wales, in the Forest Perilous, I am in dangerous territory. I recall that King Arthur enters the forest, jousting and smiting and wounding, and that the

Lady Anowrie entices him to her castle. I know I must double-check this lady, because she is a very great sorceress, and it is a relief to read that in spite of her arts, she cannot get Arthur to lie with her.

I don't look up while the suntanned guy puts his first load in the dryer and starts another in the washer. I feel confident now that the magic of the Lady Anowrie has failed, and speed up my reading a bit. The Lady Anowrie rides out into the forest with Arthur, followed by her own knights, who she has instructed to slay Arthur in revenge for scorning her. But I remember very well that Arthur is to be saved by Tristam, so race confidently towards the part where Tristam comes galloping to the rescue. But alas, as Malory is always saying, alas, I have forgotten that it is the Lady of the Lake, that friendly sorceress, who divines Arthur's danger *by her subtle crafts*, and who warns Tristam of the king's peril.

Yeah yeah. Whereas the Lady of the Lake and Tristam rode at a great pace, and were just in time – yeah yeah – to rescue Arthur from death at the hands of Anowrie and her knights.

Then King Arthur smites off the head of the Lady Anowrie, and the Lady of the Lake takes up the head and hangs it at her saddle bow by the hair, and I get up and turn off the dryer.

The washing is still a bit damp. I put in another twenty cents, then go out into the street and stand under a tristania tree, saying to myself that I have never been as bored in my life.

It is a beautiful day, with a light wind and a hot sun. There are two beaches, Bondi and Coogee, both only a bus ride away, and Wil is always saying that on the next good day we will grab a few hours and go surfing. But the good days pass, eaten up by busyness and the pranks of medieval rulers who were, actually, nothing better than Mafia bosses. I peel a hanging shred of bark from the tree, revealing the tender pinkish-tan trunk. It reminds me of the flesh of a man's back seen through a torn shirt. I go into a snap fantasy about running back into the laundromat, and bending over the suntanned guy to whisper, Let's go surfing. But I snap out as fast as I snapped in, and decide that though I shall certainly go surfing, and go today, I will go alone. I am such a weak surfer that I never go alone, so the decision is satisfactorily reckless. I shall go to Bondi, where no dragon has ever been seen rolling in on the surf, or to Coogee, where no knight in armour has ever trod.

From the door of the laundromat, the owner is calling out Miss, Miss. She is an old Japanese, and bows her head. The guy in the red shirt doesn't even look at me as I go in. While packing the laundry into its bag I burst into silent laughter. My father lives at Coogee, and I burst into this silent nervous laughter at the notion of going, of actually going, in this perfectly impulsive way, to see him.

I tell myself that it is only a notion, and that I shall go to Bondi. I buy eggs and bread and salad stuff on the way home and put them with Malory in my bag. As I pass over the money I am clumsy, and my hands jerk out of their accustomed rhythm.

There is no truck at the door. Scotty and Clark

have gone off somewhere, and in our flat the air is hot and unnaturally quiet.

I unpack the food and put it away. I put Ed's letter at Wil's end of the table. I put Malory, very neatly, at right angles, on top of my notebook. One instance of magic does not disprove a theory, and I still have the whole weekend, those two long long days.

I gobble down a cheese sandwich and a banana, walking about and dancing a bit and looking out of the window. I put a towel, my swimmies, and a tube of cream in my pack, and then, on a virtuous impulse, I deftly slide out my work notebook from under Malory and put that in too. Then I look up Huth in the phone directory.

No Huth in Coogee is listed, which means I have to get out my father's letter.

It is filed with Daddy's Biog in the filing case Gran gave me. I wonder if, like mine to Mum from Lucca, it will turn out to be milder than remembered. But no, it is still a fence of spikes. Also, I had not noticed before that he gave no phone number.

I don't withdraw my half-intention. The address is clear in my head. But I wobble.

The truth is, I am afraid, and ashamed of my fear, and if I go now, it will be to disprove my fear.

I put back the letter and get out the Biog. sheet, as if I'll find something decisive there.

DETAILS, POSSIBLY USEFUL, ABOUT YOUR FATHER.

As my attempts to inform you of these details invariably led to our estrangement, I am reduced to writing them down.

Vernon Douglas Huth, b. 1938, Adelaide, S.A.

Paternal grandparents: b. England and Germany.

Maternal grandparents: b. England and Scotland.

V.H. & C.A. met in Melbourne in 1970. C.A. later worked as secretary in Dept. of Modern History where V.H. was a lecturer.

It was generally considered that V.H.'s wide cultural interests, and his engagement in public causes, hampered his academic career.

When V.H. and C.A. met, V.H. was married to his second wife, Marcia.

V.H. had 8 (?) children.

Then, instead of bothering to explain that question mark, or saying if the count included me, she went on to name his books:

Sensible fellows, about three British philosophers (named) and *Mr mother country*.

Which I showed, or rather, tried to show to you.

I believe (she concluded) that V.H. would agree to add to these details, if you should condescend to see him, which would be an easy matter, now that he has moved to Sydney.

Well, I don't find anything decisive, or reassuring either, in any of this. From memory, she gave it to me when I was about seventeen. I slip it back into the H file, and am wobbling even more, when the phone rings. I expect it to be Wil to ask about the drilling on

Saturday, but it turns out to be Aunt Gail.

'CEC, SORRY to interrupt.'

I panic. Eugene has rung them. She will demand to know why I got Susan Wu's name wrong. I say meekly, 'That's okay, Auntie Gail.'

'I forgot TO TELL YOU. The Huths HAVE AN UNLISTED NUMBER.'

I gape. What else has she divined by her subtle crafts? 'Aunt Gail,' I say, in a low voice, 'I don't want it.'

'Have you A PEN THERE.'

'Sorry, Aunt Gail. Goodbye.'

I hang up, and am instantly light-hearted. I will go to Bondi. Everyone knows the surf is better at Bondi. I grab my pack, and in a minute am running down the stairs.

Scotty and Clark are crossing the footpath from their truck.

'Ay,' they call out, 'all clear now.'

'Drilling all over.'

'Ended. Finito. Done.'

'Don't care.' I give a careless wave. 'Going to Bondi.'

'Half your luck.'

'Catch one for us.'

I get a 438 bus up to Town Hall, then cross George and walk up Park towards Elizabeth. At the corner of Castlereagh and Park, I run across against the red light as the vehicles banked up on the other side of Park begin the crossing. At the very front of these, the 304 to Coogee is moving with majesty towards me. On Castlereagh I trot beside it and hop on just as the doors shut.

It is about half-full. I go towards the back and plop down with a histrionic gasp.

I stare for a while out of the window. Coogee buses are frequent. No subtle craft was needed to make the 304 crossing over Park coincide with mine over Castlereagh.

Also, going to Coogee commits me to nothing. ONE: there is surf at Coogee. TWO: my father can be visited at Coogee. But ONE is my primary objective, and shall not be sacrificed to make time for TWO.

Pact, I say to myself. The very word gives me a settled feeling. Katie and I were stern about keeping our pacts. We were like Arthur's knights, and considered ourselves vile miscreants when we broke them. I get busy and take out my notebook and pen.

At the back, three grommet types are talking surf. I've seen them all on campus somewhere. They're talking about wild chops, tight arcs, and tucking into barrels. These words are just comprehensible enough to be distracting. I take my pack and notebook to the front.

In this notebook are all my notes on Malory, beginning with earlier projects and ideas, and only gradually settling on Arthur. I've never read it consecutively before, and am surprised to find that the interest in Arthur was there from the start, and is continuous and accumulative, as if he were always my choice, but hidden from myself.

Yet, I tell myself, it is sensible to consider an alternative. It suits me that the 304 goes the long way round. I start at the beginning, putting light little ticks and crosses in the margins. In Surry Hills, I look up at the corner of the street where Katie used to live with Sean, and where Sean still lives. I watch for a block, in case I see him coming out of one of the little shops. Chun-Ling, of course, still lives with her parents.

I reject the threatened intrusion of Eugene and Susan Wu, and go back to my notes. I take care. I concentrate. Shadows of plane trees fall across the pages as we pass through the little old streets. Sunlight falls on the pages as we race through the wide parks. I don't even raise my head until the hills become steep and the descents abrupt, and I am conscious of old people lurching and staggering as they rise to get out, and I don't put the notebook back till we stop in Beach Street.

I hurry down the hill to the beach. The three grommet types are behind me. At the corner a wind strikes me. No longer the light wind I felt outside the laundromat, but a good one, strong and steady. The grommet types pass me, saying excitedly that that's a south-westerly.

'Real resistance in that.'

'Be some green rooms in there.'

They run ahead. I follow slowly. The only time I was in one of those green rooms the Pacific Ocean was trying to batter its way into every orifice in my head. I remember very clearly my long hoarse breaths as I walked up the beach after my escape, my rasping chest held between my forward hanging arms, the full female chimpanzee. I go slowly across the grass, looking sideways at the bay, where the wind and tide are fighting it out. On the rocky obstacle of Wedding Cake Island the ocean dashes and seethes and tosses up huge arches of spray. It looks very desperate to me. But at the same time I feel that deep thrilling oceanic embrace, and I walk quick and buoyant yet undecided down the shallow crescent-shaped steps to the beach.

Then I notice that not all the people walking away from the surf are middle-aged or old, or mothers with children. Some are young, and some look truc-ulent. A couple of boys are coming my way, one dark, about eighteen, carrying a broken board, the other younger, flaxen-haired, his board undamaged. Both wear the beautiful knee-length armour of the grommets, black and glistening and stabbed and banded with bright electrical colour.

I speak to the dark one. 'Why aren't there more people in?'

He considers me. The fair one looks out to sea, where a blue container ship moves calmly on the horizon.

'Is it dangerous or something?' I ask.

'I don't know about dangerous,' says the dark one.

'What then?' I ask.

'Shane here got into trouble.'

He doesn't say this to me, but to the fair boy, who instantly turns round and blurts out at him, 'Ar, Johnny, fucken wind turned cross-shore.'

'Certainly did,' says Johnny, with a lilt. And now he addresses me. 'Wave faces got real bumpy. Got in a bit of trouble myself.'

'All I want to do,' I say doubtfully, 'is to play around inshore.'

'Please yourself,' says Johnny, with his lilt. 'But you can get sliced even inshore. Fact is, there's a lot of ignorant lunatics out there. Some kind of university vacation, they tell me.'

'Oh?' I say. 'Well, thanks. I suppose it'll have to be Wylie's Baths.'

'They're shut,' shouts Shane triumphantly, again addressing Johnny.

'Why?' I ask with indignation.

'Don't know,' says Johnny, shrugging.

'Well, thank you,' I say, in a thanks-for-nothing tone.

They turn to go. My heart is beating fast. I have, after all, made a pact with myself, and Wylie's Baths, in any case, would have been a shameful compromise. I run after Johnny and Shane.

'Hey!' I say to Johnny, 'You know where Foss Street is?'

'Sure,' he says. 'Come and I'll show you.'

He is friendly now. He and I cross the grass towards Arden Street, Shane in the rear.

'They're making these boards too thin,' confides Johnny.

'They look thin,' I say.

'Coogee's not my scene. North's my scene. I only come here for Shane. To teach him. You know someone up Foss Street?'

'Sort-of,' I say.

We reach the footpath of Arden Street. He points. 'Up there, and then to the left.'

Coogee Beach lies between two peaked headlands. I have to drop my head right back to follow his pointing finger. And my heart, as Malory would say, misgave me. 'How far up?' I ask.

'Way-way up. Last on the left.'

Shane, who has caught up with us, though not right up, gives a laugh. Johnny says to me, 'You got a car?'

'No.' I grasp the straps of my pack and say, 'But I've walked worse than that.'

Johnny is still pointing. 'Shane'll run you up.'

Shane makes a choking noise. Johnny stops pointing and turns to face him. Shane looks far out to sea. He looks at the blue container ship on the horizon. A flush of red moves from the shining black and ultramarine of his wetsuit, up the sinews and flesh of his neck, and into his averted face.

'What?' I say, friendly. 'You have a car, Shane?'

'Bike,' says Johnny. Shane doesn't turn his head. The blush looks purplish as it moves into his flaxen hair.

'Listen,' I say in a low voice to Johnny, 'I can walk.'

'Wait,' says Johnny. He commandingly touches my shoulder as he passes me and goes to Shane. Shane doesn't move. Johnny bows his head over Shane's head and makes a hissing noise. Shane still doesn't move. Johnny stands over him, with this hiss, then waits, then hisses again. He waits again. And suddenly, Shane turns to me and croaks desperately, 'I'll run you up.'

Johnny claps a hand on Shane's shoulder. 'He'll run

you up,' he tells me. He clasps Shane's shoulder, very friendly, and gives it a shake. Then he releases him and moves off. With two fingers high above his head, he waves to us both.

'See ya!'

Somebody has to break the silence. 'Your friend Johnny,' I say to Shane, 'is a very great magician.'

I hate myself when I talk in this privately joking way. It's all right with someone as strong as you are, with Aunt Gail, say, but with someone like Shane, who is too shy even to look at you, and whose arms, as he shifts his board, seem fractured with awkwardness, it's condescending. So it surprises me when he speaks, though without looking at me.

'You're not wrong.'

Avoiding obvious kindness, I sound curt. 'Where's your bike?'

'Behind my Uncle's shop.'

He still won't look at me, but at least we are speaking. Perhaps he feels freer when released from Johnny's expectations, or not overwhelmed by Johnny's example. As we cross Arden Street I say, 'I said that about magic because of the way he hissed at you.'

This startles him into giving me a quick look. 'He didn't hiss.'

'What did he do, then?'

But Shane won't tell me. He looks away. His walk is an ungainly trudge.

'Where's your Uncle's shop?'

'Just round there.'

And he gives a fairly wild sideways wave. It annoys me that he walks slightly ahead of me, and looks away all the time, but I refuse to make this an excuse to give up, and doggedly follow. We enter a lane beside a hardware shop, and he rings a bell beside a black door.

'What sort of a bike?' I ask, for something to say.

'Suzuki.'

A big middle-aged man opens the door, gestures okay, and hurries away through an opposite door into the shop. We are in the shop's store room, and the Suzuki is propped near the door. Shane mumbles, 'Excuse me,' and disappears through a third door in the right-hand wall.

Almost at once, the man appears in the door to the shop.

'You riding with Shane?'

'Yes. To Foss Street.'

'Ah.' He nods in understanding. 'Johnny told him to take you.'

'More or less.'

He nods again. 'You know Shane hasn't a licence yet?'

'I wondered.'

'But it's fair enough to say this. I wouldn't let him ride that thing if he wasn't competent. It's mine. But Shane, he was mustering sheep on those things when he was twelve.'

'I see. A country boy.'

'Not any more he's not. He's going for a change of element. Land to water. An apprentice grommet now.' He glances at the bike again, turns one hand upwards, and says, 'Well, it's up to you. But don't forget those.'

He points to two helmets on a shelf, then disappears. I hear a toilet flush. I stand perfectly still, grasping the straps of my pack and staring into the shop, where a woman is wandering slantwise along a row of shelves. An unlicensed rider is the perfect excuse to change my mind, to escape, to walk out of the door, to run across Arden Street, to hop on one of the swift buses and open my notebook. In the tension of that moment, I don't question why the option of riding on that bike up to Foss Street has demolished the option of walking. In fact, it seems that this last perfect excuse to avoid confronting my father can only be a test of strength of my resolve to keep my pact.

Shane comes out. He looks smaller without his armour. His flaxen hair is wet and combed. He is dressed in blue jeans, a white T-shirt, and white runners. He doesn't look at me. He goes straight to the bike, opens the panel-thing covering the engine, and starts doing something to something.

Then, from the safety of this busy-ness, he speaks, distantly but clearly.

'That was the name of two girls,' he says, 'what you called hissing.'

'Oh,' I say, 'I see.'

I do see, too. The little details, moving easily into place, confirm Johnny's method of working on Shane's shyness.

'Girls you like,' I say.

'Used to,' he says stoically to the engine.

'What, Louisa and Esther?'

'No.' He looks up. He actually looks straight at

149

me. He laughs. 'Hester and Marissa.'

I laugh too. 'And Hester and Marissa were mean?'

'It wasn't their fault,' he says, quite aggressive. 'They were gorgeous. You can't blame them.'

'Well, I wasn't.'

'Not when I didn't have a word to say.'

'But that's amazing, Shane,' I say. 'Look at you now. Talking away like anything. You're all right now.'

'Yeah.' He looks pleased. 'Johnny was right. He said to practise on older girls, who don't matter.'

'Good idea. And,' I say, surprising myself by my mother's voice, 'it might be another good idea if you were not to tell people they don't matter.'

'I only meant not mattering in that way.'

'I know. But just as a general rule, see?'

'Yeah,' he says, with languid hostility. But then he says Yeah again, comprehending now. 'That's right,' he says. 'That's good advice. And Johnny's right, too. Because, look, how am I going to get on, I mean, even apart from that, I mean, in business and everything, if I can't, you know, say a word?'

'How indeed?' I say, again with my mother's coolness, her distance, her exact intonation.

Shane hands me a helmet, and says, as he puts the other one on, 'I mean, if you're not, you know, brave enough.'

'You've simply got to be,' I tell us both.

'Well, right, come on,' he says with authority. He trundles the bike to the door. 'And listen, I'm telling you, when we get to that hill, you hang on real tight.'

150

Shane's uncle must either have devoted himself too ardently to his nephew's confidence-building, or have been too busy in the shop to watch him riding through traffic. Shane was not used to obstacles that did not instantly make way for him, as in fact these (one just in time) did. It is true that once we reached the hill, which by luck was obstacle free, he roared up in an absolutely straight and glorious burst, while alongside us raced an exploding strip of sun and ocean and green or rocky headland. I hung on, as I had been told to, real tight, and fear flew away as my arms around his body transmitted to my body his triumph and joy. And he slowed down at the top nicely and smoothly too.

'Foss Street,' he says, jerking his head. 'Want me to run you in?'

Foss Street looks scarcely more than a leafy lane. 'Not a worry,' I say, getting off.

I find that my legs are trembling, but now that it is over, and I am alive, there is no point in spoiling the contribution I have made towards Shane's confidence. So I take off the helmet, and smile as I give it to him, and say, 'Thanks a lot Shane,' and then give that sideways nod of approbation.

He is so pleased that his smile is almost galvanic. No doubt this is the moment to add a few responsible words about looking out for the traffic down there, but I have too much ahead of me to bother, so I turn away waving and calling good-bye as blithely as Marie Antoinette telling them to eat cake, and as I enter Foss Street I scarcely notice the receding roar of his descent.

It is hard for me, now, to believe that until I walked into Foss Street, I never imagined that Vernon Huth would not be at home. I don't know why I didn't remind myself that a lecturer in modern history, even during stu-vac, would be likely to be in his department. But that was how it was. I just didn't. The reason is probably my egotism, or what Aunt Gail calls my self-absorption, though an alternative could be an underlying obedience to her magic, deployed in this case in that noon phone call. Anyway, for whatever reason, I took it for granted that to walk into Foss Street, to enter the gate of No. 3, smartly clicking it behind me, to walk to the door and ring the bell, would certainly mean that I would be led to him. And that the leading would be done by Kirsty the sweet thing. And it is also possible that it was Aunt Gail's pronouncement on Kirsty's sweetness that made me brave enough, when actually in Foss Street, to go on.

Foss Street is the kind of rugged terrain where there are houses on only one side, all half-hidden by trees and shrubs and outcrops of rock. I pass the first house, a salt-pitted old brick bungalow, then another one the same, but now restored and glassy, with a carport at street level among the trees, and then, also at street level (if you can call it a street, and call it level), a garage stuck up on stilts, and beyond it, what looks like a vacant scrubby slope until I see a red roof down there, plus a bit of wall, white. There is no fence, but I see a short post, and on this post a big letter box, and on the letter box a big blue 3.

'Arrivo,' I whisper, as I had done when seeing

the number on the Ambrussi house at Lucca. And as I had not whispered or said Arrivo since then, I realise now that it might have been in hidden fear of a similar hostility.

I emerge from the shelter of the garage and go and stand by the post. From here I see a rough path leading down to what must be the house, and beside this path a woman is standing with her legs wide apart and bending so low that her two iron-grey plaits are actually touching the earth, out of which she is trying to pull something resistant. She is trying very hard. I hear her panting and saying Shit. The visible parts of her dress are blackish and printed with big arrowheads of copper and blue.

As Aunt Gail's pronouncement that Kirsty was a sweet thing had made me imagine her as plump and somehow supplicating, and dressed in a Liberty cotton frock, maybe with pintucks, I think this squaw woman can't possibly be her, so I just stand there, stupidly staring. Also, I had rather counted on that clicking gate, that ringing bell, to announce me, and now that I must announce myself, and try a feeble cough, my throat goes dry.

But I must have made some small noise, or she may have felt my presence, because she suddenly straightens her back, and at the same time tosses back her plaits and is looking right up at me.

'Oh,' she says, loud enough to reach me up there, hanging onto the post. 'You're Cecily. Good. You've come. I'm Kirsty.'

I feel the blush rising up my neck and into my face. I am blushing like Shane. Kirsty gives me the quickest of glances, then looks casually away, raises her right arm to shoulder level, and, with palm downwards, swings it around.

'All this,' she says, 'was lantana.'

I know she is giving me time to recover. 'And every scrap of it,' she says, still indicating with her sweeping arm the earth around her, 'must come out.'

'Why?' I blurt out.

'Why?' She drops her arm. She looks at me and smiles.

'Yes, why?' I say. 'I love lantana.'

'Oh no, you don't.' She speaks affectionately, almost caressingly. 'You can't possibly. It's my enemy.'

'I love the scent,' I say.

'Oh no,' she says. Now she is taking handfuls of something from a pocket. These turn out to be hairpins and as she speaks, she quickly gathers and pins her plaits to the back of her head, her eyes all the time looking up at me. 'It's the purple lantana you like the scent of,' she says. 'So do I. That's the garden lantana. But this is the suffocating bush stuff. You can't like this.'

'I like it,' I say, starting down the rough path, 'in its place.'

She laughs again and looks at me as I pick my way down the path. Her dress is a beautiful loose garment and the broad blunt arrowheads are woven into the cloth. She looks a good bit older than Aunt Gail. Her skin is brown and lined, and her eyes, narrow and dark and bright, are watching me with shrewdness and frank curiosity.

I find I am at ease. I receive the strongest possible impression, like an emanation, of her intrinsic honesty. Though not honest myself, I love honest people, and find the air around them somehow easier to breathe.

I say, 'Why don't you poison it?'

'I am trying not to,' she says.

'Even my mother,' I say, 'had to use poison.'

'Was it lantana?'

'I think it was privet.'

This is a kind of comfortable, almost absent-minded exchange. We are not really talking about privet and lantana, but are making time to look at each other. She smiles and says, 'Well *my* mother assures me it will come to that. Do you want to see Vernon?'

'He's home, then?' I say.

'Oh yes, he's home.' She turns up the palms of her hands and looks at them. 'Come and we'll wash these, and then we'll go in.'

She leads the way across the rough earth until we join a flight of new concrete steps which, I see now, lead from the garage to the house. I address my words to the mass of iron grey hair heaped on her head. 'Were you really at school with Aunt Gail?'

'Is that what she said? I was leaving just as she was starting. My first sight of her was standing in the playground screaming her head off. Her first day, poor little thing, she hated it.'

We have turned into a laundry, also new. 'Not for long, I bet,' I say.

'No. She was so pretty and clever, she was a great success. She says now I rescued her, that first day. But my memory of it is that everyone was running to rescue her.'

She is washing her hands, looking at me side-ways with her benevolent curiosity. 'You sounded surprised that your father is home.'

'I thought he might be at work.'

'He has no work.' She pulls a towel from the rod without looking away from my face. 'Didn't Gail tell you he got the sack?'

I shake my head. 'Well,' she says, 'that's what happened. And that's what he calls it. The sack. He won't have any talk of redundancy or packages. Oh, it was a long and hard-fought business, believe me. But perhaps all that didn't register with Gail.'

'She is so busy.'

'That's true, poor dear. But when I say Vernon has no work, please don't think he's idle. He is to do an expanded version of his first book. At a publisher's suggestion. He has a contract. He has begun to rationalise his material –' She puts a hand on my back and ushers me through a door '– and in the New Year he will start.'

We are passing through a long narrow larder, its shelves packed as logically as in a shop, and now she ushers me into a hall, and after a few paces we halt at the open door of a big bright kitchen. An old woman with straight white bobbed hair stands near the fridge, and a boy and a girl, eighteen-ish, sit at the table drinking from mugs, both with books in front of them.

'This is Cecily,' says Kirsty, 'Cecily, this is my mother, Janet Canning. And these two are Robert and Clare.'

'Bob,' mutters Robert, and Clare mutters something like Hello. I say Hello just as indifferently, and avoid looking at them. I wonder if they are my half-siblings, but that's not an aspect of the matter I'm ready to examine, or encourage any emotion about. And for whatever reason, they have the same air of avoidance that I have, and I am glad that Kirsty's hand is on my back, and that she is talking across the kitchen to her mother.

'Cecily tells me I should poison it too.'

The old woman quietly laughs. She is unusually tall, and holds her forearms at chest level, with her little hands curled over, like a kangaroo. 'One of those systemic poisons,' she says with satisfaction.

'I suppose I'll come to it in the end,' says Kirsty. 'Do you want coffee or anything, Cecily?'

'No thanks,' I say, low and humble and very nervous.

'Come along then. Oh, but do leave your pack here.'

I prop the pack just inside the door. Robert and Clare don't look up from their books. Janet Canning stands with her little kangaroo paws curled and calls out something humorous about spades and mattocks. Kirsty and I walk down the hall, then start up a flight of steps.

Like the outdoor steps, these steps are new. You can almost smell the new wood. They are simple timber treads, curving half-way up. I look at

Kirsty's back, and wish I had worn my Indian shirt, which is a kind of poor relation in the same international family as her beautiful dress. I even remind myself to ask where she got it. In the dentist's chair, I always concentrate on designing a delicious meal I shall eat that night.

Until I was four, I didn't ask about my father. Or if I did, I don't remember it. (I still believe that when I was very small, Gran told me he was dead, though of course she denies it.) I can't recall, either, how old I was when Mum told me his name and occupation, and that she once worked for him. Nor do I recall how long it was after that when Katie and I read a novel about a woman who had a daughter by a garbage collector, and because she wanted to bestow upon this daughter a more elevated idea of herself, she named as her father the mayor of the town. Katie and I, with varying degrees of hilarity, made a case for Mum having done the same thing, and after we had enough of the details in place, such as substituting a janitor for the garbage collector, I went and accused Mum of it. It was then that she showed me Vernon Huth's photograph on the jacket flap of his little book on James Stephen. The photograph was of a man with a beard. When she asked if I couldn't see the resemblance, I said maybe I would see it when I grew a beard (storing this away for Katie), and she said, 'Please study the proportions. Look at the angle of the temple to the frontal bone. Look at the eye sockets, and the setting of the ears.' And when I could no longer deny the resemblance, I held the photograph an inch from my eyes, and giggled and said it was too tiny. She asked if I would like a blown-up copy, and I laughed and said, No thanks, and threw the jacket down and danced away. She had already told me that he had refused to know me, and my dancing away, and my jokes, and my delirious fabrications with Katie disguised my deep offendedness and hostility, compounded of course by his silence over the years and recently confirmed by his crabby letter.

The door we halt at is also new, and Kirsty opens it just enough to put her head in. 'Vern,' I hear her say, in a smiling voice, 'Cecily's here.'

I hear a shuffle, an exclamation, and then Kirsty says, 'No, I mean she's standing beside me, here. Right now.' And she opens the door, and I follow her in.

It is a biggish room, new and light and glassy. At a right angle to one wall is a desk, behind which my father is standing with his fingertips tautly pressed on the top, among many piles of papers.

'Great God,' he is muttering. 'Great God.'

My throat has gone dry again. I am not blushing, but perhaps I will faint. Kirsty puts an arm round me and says, 'I told you she would come. Gail said so.'

I am so stupid that I suspect only then that my aunt-by-marriage has engineered this visit to get me to lay off Uncle Nick. My father is still standing as if petrified, and still muttering Great God, and as I now feel that I might wet my pants, I say desperately, 'You've shaved off your beard.'

He puts one hand to his face, and touches his cheeks, all over. 'But,' he says dreamily, 'that was years ago.'

Suddenly Kirsty points to the desk. 'Look at it, Cec,' she says loudly. She advances on it, and I go with her, for safety's sake. 'Look at it. I know it's a flaw in my character, but I can't bear to look at a mess like that without itching to tidy it up. I hope you're not like that, Cec.'

I say that I am, a bit, and at the same time my father says coyly that it's not as bad as it looks, and that he knows where everything is.

'I don't believe it.' Kirsty, in contrast to the two dummies she is trying to animate, is all drama and laughter. 'Anyway, it's the look of the thing I can't bear. I can't. I'll have to run away.'

And she does that, not exactly running, but walking fast, and waving a hand, and laughing, and saying she'll see me later. And as it would be too pathetic, even for me, to run after her, I stand there watching Vernon Huth shifting his paper weights around.

Every pile of paper is weighted: with a small brass elephant, a river pebble, a pottery apple, a magnet, a bronze Buddha, and so on. And he is moving these about and swapping one for another as if playing a board game, while saying, 'Kirsty knows very well, she knows very well, that as soon as Jerome can come, all this, all this, will go on disc.'

I haven't the least idea who Jerome is. I wonder if I shall ever know who Jerome is. I pick up the pottery apple. 'This is lovely,' I say politely.

He grabs it from me, but only so that he can offer it.

'Take it,' he says forcibly. 'It's yours.'

I take it and turn it round in my fingers. It is glazed with great skill, and is clearly identifiable as a Jonathan apple. We are both still standing. I put it back on its papers and wander away from the desk, looking all around me: carefully at the bookshelves (history, myth, philosophy, film), casually at the shelves of discs by the word processor, critically at the lighting fixtures. I am aware that Vernon Huth has left the desk and is hovering, rather like a real estate agent letting the client have a good look first. I wander to the big windows, where I come to a stop and say graciously, 'What a magnificent view.'

'Isn't it!' He comes bustling up behind me. 'That's what we fell in love with. You see that from all the back rooms. That's what made us buy the wreck of a place.'

And now my eyes catch up with my social intention and I see that it really is magnificent. Below the steeply falling land, below the tops of squat palms, hibiscus, casuarina, and a lemon tree, below the carton and the plastic bag lodged in a sidling canopy of morning glory, there is no beach, but only a rocky pointed little bay. I look far down upon the backs of seagulls skimming foamy waves. I look forward across the mass of the ocean to the delicate horizon and the sky, the sky, the sky.

Covetousness rises, a mere whiff. 'We'll be renovating,' Vernon Huth is saying glumly, 'for the rest of our lives.'

'Yes,' I say.

'But it's the perfect aspect, that north-east.'

I was so amazed to have a father who doesn't know the compass points that before I can stop myself I am pointing and saying, 'But that's east-north-east.'

He is silent. I hear a plane approaching. I look at the unoccupied sky, then take a sidelong look at him and see him looking in the same sneaky startled way at me.

'There's quite a resemblance,' he says.

'Some,' I say.

'I meant to Chris, too.' He raises his voice against the noise of the approaching plane. 'But the physical resemblance to me, well it's remarkable.'

'Not in the circumstances,' I say.

'I never denied it, you know.'

I give a shrug. The huge plane has entered the frame and is passing sluggishly across the sky. 'We weren't under the flight path when we bought,' shouts my father.

I watch the plane.

'They changed it, they changed it.' I believe he will now shake his fist at the plane, but instead he says crossly, 'Oh, but look, come and sit down.'

He leads the way. He is not a tall man, and we are alike even in the way we move. His grey hair is as frizzy and almost as thick as mine. He is wearing new white Reeboks, and I visualise, resting on the reinforcement of their soles, and nestling in their padding and swaddling, his pretty pearly little feet.

'My cousin –' I say.

But he is pulling his swivel chair free of the desk. At least he doesn't intend to sit behind the desk as if interviewing me. He wheels the chair to the end of the desk, then positions a second chair approximately to face it. 'Your cousin?' he says, indicating with a hand that the second chair is for me.

'My cousin in Melbourne –' I say, sitting down.

He sits in the swivel chair, with an elbow on the desk awkwardly nudging the pile of papers weighted by the brass elephant. 'Now which cousin is that?' he asks fussily.

'The only one I know of. Eugene Ambruss. You've met Aunt Gail.'

'Oh Gail, Gail. Recently, yes.'

'Well, her son. He knows someone who saw you last week, walking over Princes Bridge –'

'Oh-Oh.' He is laughing. 'Oh-Oh. That?'

'Yes. Where were your shoes?'

'Oh-Oh. One of those lads had them in his bag. And gave them to me on the city side. But they spoilt it, you know, the ones who gathered round like that, laughing. Its effect depended on it being absolutely dead-pan. I was demonstrating, or trying to, the kind of humour that derives entirely from unexpected juxtaposition.'

I had noticed, in my strolling survey of his bookshelves, in the books on film, the recurring name of Bunuel. 'Like in Bunuel?' I say.

'*Very* good,' he says, as if commending a student. 'You like Bunuel?'

'I haven't seen much of him,' I say, 'but when he makes me laugh, yes.'

163

'I wrote a monograph on him. Unhappily, nobody has seen fit to publish it. But that incident on Princes Bridge. That wasn't last week. That was September. I was down there speaking at a conference. For a decent fee, I need hardly add.'

He picks up the little elephant and mutters something about every penny he can get. Then he says, remote yet chatty, turning the elephant in his hand, 'Your mother was a lovely woman. When I first saw her, I thought she may have been a dancer. Her height, you know, her grace, the way she pulled that magnificent hair so severely back. And those black clothes she favoured. Yes, worn with those rather luxurious silk scarves.'

I want to say that those two silk scarves were still in the house when she died, but he goes on.

'Those scarves she bought in India. Did she see much of Gerard Scott?'

'Scutt,' I say.

'Scutt, was it? Fellow she travelled to India with. I thought there might be something doing there.'

'He used to turn up now and then.'

'I've wondered.'

He looks at the little elephant. The silence becomes irksome, yet now we seem trapped in chat-mode, and when I break the silence, I have to say, with the same bright neutrality, 'Kirsty tells me you're rationalising your material.'

He gives a sidelong glance at his desk. Then, delicately, he stands the little elephant back in place and says, 'I thought I might as well give it a go.' He raises one eyebrow and scratches with a forefinger the temple beside it. 'Since they asked me so nicely, and gave me a contract. Yes indeed. And I can't claim to be short of time. Of course you know I got the sack.'

'I didn't. Kirsty just told me.'

He looked so surprised that I now suspect him of being egotistical enough to assume all his affairs to be public knowledge. 'I've been living a very narrow life lately,' I am kind enough to add.

I am about to renew my attack on chat-mode by going on to say, 'Since Mum died, and my friends disbanded,' when he attacks it himself by saying, 'Oh yes, they dumped me, gave me the old heave-ho, gave me the boot, kicked me out. Yes, against all my resistance. I wouldn't go on about this if it weren't relevant to what you want to talk about. I beg your pardon, what I assume you want to talk about. My bad-tempered letter to you. That's it?'

I say, 'Well,' but before I can say I don't know, as precisely as all that, what I want to talk about, he goes on again.

'I was in the thick of that fight, you see. And it was a fight. Oh yes, I fought them. And there I was, in the thick of it, as I said, when I got Nick Ambruss's letter telling me of Chris's death, and suggesting I write to you. Now, consider the timing. I was angry. Not with your uncle. Not with you. Certainly not. I mean that anger was the climate I was living in. Anger was the air I was breathing. I put off replying, and Kirsty kept reminding me, which didn't improve my temper – please don't think I'm proud of this – and then one day I dashed off something, I hardly knew what. And then you replied, as casual and nonchalant as could be. So I thought, Well, sensible girl, that's that. But it left a trace of uneasiness, which by and by started to grow hands and feet, and got uncomfortable, then distinctly uncomfortable. And then one day, after I had accepted, had begun to accept, what they had done to me, in what I consider the prime of my life, I showed your letter to Kirsty, and she suggested that the nonchalance was bravado.'

He pauses. He looks straight at me. 'Was it?'

The nearest paper weight is the pottery apple. I pick it up. But my hand trembles. I put it down and say, 'Anger.'

'Oh,' he says.

'Also offence.'

'Well,' he says, 'I mentioned the resemblance.'

We survey each other for a moment. Then he points at me and says, 'There was another distraction when I wrote to you. You may think it too trivial to mention, yet it had its influence. Again, I must ask you to consider the timing. We had just moved in here, you understand, and at just that time, they chose to change the flight path. And at just that time also, the contractors began work on the side steps and the laundry. Now, as everybody knows, building contractors are very important people, and their will cannot be gainsaid. So, concrete mixers. So, electric drills. Oh, I know, I know,' he says, as I widen my eyes, 'I know how it sounds. I said it was trivial. But its effect on me was not. It was – please try to understand – the last, unbearable thing. And no escape, any more, to a nice quiet room in the university. Those drills, they were drilling that message into my beleaguered brain.'

'Some people use muffling devices,' I say.

'Oh, don't imagine I didn't try those. But perhaps I ought to mention a few other events at that time. Hardly worth mentioning, I realise that, such as a son smashing up my car, such as a daughter getting pregnant. I know I shouldn't have allowed those events, all or any of them, to influence what I wrote to you. But there you are, I did, and I'm sorry.'

And now I want to reply that when I replied I was also living in a climate of anger. Anger and grief. I want to mention grief as a means of bringing my mother back into the conversation. But instead, it turns out to be one of those times when my right hand doesn't know what the left is doing, and I come out with one of those unpremeditated things.

'Exactly how many children have you?'

'Ah now,' he says, 'don't let us start on that.'

'As one of them, I believe I'm entitled to know.'

'Entitlements,' he says, with theatrical weariness. 'All these entitlements.'

He is fiddling with the nearest pile of papers now, riffling the edges and so on. 'Well, of course I'll tell you,' he says. 'I'll tell you that. But first I would like you to tell me something, surely relevant to what you've come about. Which, if it isn't about my letter, is about my relationship with Chris?'

I can't deny it. 'Or perhaps,' he says, '*also* about my relationship with your mother. Yes?'

'Yes,' he replies to himself, without even looking at

me. 'Yes. Well, you were in a state of anger when you replied to my letter. But also you were, like me, in a state of grief. And I am not so crass as to fail to realise that your grief was of a more primal sort than mine. You were grieving for your mother. But you were angry too. And, I gather, not only with me, but about a clause in her will.'

He raises a hand when I try to speak. He lowers his eyelids and says, 'Please.' He gives me a few seconds, repeats Please, then opens his eyes and says quietly, 'We will come to your question, I promise you. But I want to say this thing while I remember it. Yes, about that marriage clause. Your partner, I believe, is a very fine and brilliant fellow. I'm sorry, I've forgotten his name.'

'His name is Wilfred Bonar Meade,' I say, 'and Aunt Gail thinks I ought to obey my mother and marry him immediately. And evidently you think so too. And it's true that he's a very fine and brilliant fellow. In fact, he's too good for me.'

'Too good in what way?' asks my father.

'Too virtuous,' I say.

'Oh-oh. Well, Kirsty's too virtuous for me. Yet we get on. It's not a bad thing. It trims the boat. But that's beside the point. This is what I want to say, before we embark on anything more contentious. No doubt your Wil is very fine, and no doubt you love him. But why take any action at all? Consider this. You are that most fortunate of human creatures, a healthy young person with an adequate intelligence and a small private income. What a base that is, what an enviable base to work from!'

I am disconcerted by this expression of what my own instinct tells me when undiverted by the opinion of others. I gave him a few rapid blinks and say abruptly, 'Yes, but what made her do it?'

'What? But surely all the world knows that mothers want their daughters to be safe. It's an instinct nearly as strong as the breeding instinct itself. And I gather that Chris had met Wil, and was very much impressed.'

Of course, other people have offered the same simple explanation: Carmen and Sandra, Mr Parry, Uncle Nick, and Rachel. So perhaps my readiness to accept it now is only because of its accumulated weight. I don't want to begin to like my father, or to be impressed by his opinions. I get a glimmering of my reason for coming today.

'Well,' I say, 'you've had some experience of mothers. Tell me, how many mothers have your undisclosed number of children had?'

He stares at me, full on. I suppose age decreases the tendency to blush, but his skin goes slightly red. 'Cecily,' he says, 'would you like a cup of coffee?'

'No thank you,' I say. Daddy, I add to myself.

'I've a coffee maker over there.' He is pointing to the opposite wall.

'No thank you,' I repeat.

'Well,' he says, sighing and restoring his elbow to its awkward place among the papers. 'I know most people find this very amusing, this story of the campaigner for population control with so many children of his own. And that central fact is that

Marcia, my second wife, was one of those women who realised, at some time during her first pregnancy, or perhaps during the first birth, that she had struck her metier. Yes, her metier. She was an artist, you see, an artist in child-bearing. And there's no stopping artists once they strike their metier. They'll employ any method, any deceit. And sometimes, this is the incredible thing, not even know they're doing it.'

He stops abruptly, and stares at me with what looks like accusation. 'I hope you're not an artist.'

'Please,' I say, 'go on with what you were telling me.'

'Of course. Your question. How many mothers have my children had? Two mothers. My first wife died, of natural causes, strangely enough, leaving twins. So, now, the children, that makes, let me see, yes, nine.'

'Am I included in that count?'

'I'm sorry, I should have said ten.' He looks longingly at the opposite wall. 'There's mineral water,' he says, 'or fruit juice.'

'No thank you,' I say.

'Of course, as you are thinking, and as your mother pointed out, I could have done something myself to stem the tide. I mean sterilisation, of course. I admit I hesitated.'

'I expect you would,' I say.

But if he notices my tone, he is too heated to care.

'But I did it. I did it. And left Marcia also. Charming, as I have never denied. A very beautiful and charming woman. But too wilfully fecund for me. Too fecund for my beliefs, my emotions, and my income. I had a right to an opinion in the matter. Shall we call it an entitlement? Yes. And that was it. That was my opinion. I planned a divorce. I wanted to marry or live with Christina Ambruss. I thought it would be like living in bracing mountain air after the swampy coast. Well, consider my feelings when Christina Ambruss told me she was pregnant, having slotted one in, to use her exact words, just before I had the job done. Did she ever tell you that?'

I can't speak. I shake my head.

'Ashamed,' he says, 'Ashamed. And so she ought to have been. I couldn't forgive her. I didn't deny paternity, but I told her that if she persisted in the pregnancy, there would be no willing help from me, and no contact of any kind. Did she care? Not a bit. She packed up and went to Sydney with two friends. Keen skinny beady-eyed types, both in the same boat.'

'Carmen and Sandra,' I say.

'Something like that.'

'I gave them those scarves, one each.'

'Indeed.'

Though his voice is cold, his eyes, resting on my face, are, for the first time, gentle.

'Things might have been different, you know, if Chris had stayed in Melbourne, and I had seen you as a child. You get fond of them, you can't help it. Oh, but also,' he says, dry again, 'things might have been different if Marcia hadn't also slotted one in. A boy. Well, she wanted another boy. Like a painter, you know, needing a little more weight at the base, or a composer deciding on a coda.'

'I see this information impresses you,' he then says, accurately enough. 'As for me, these are incidents I don't willingly revive. I find them very disturbing. As you see. As you see. I loved your mother. But I couldn't forgive her for that. It was the most high-handed thing I've ever encountered in my life.'

'High-handed,' I repeat the word after him. It brings us almost into conspiracy. 'High-handed. That describes exactly what she did to me.'

'You refer to that marriage clause?'

'Not only to that. Aunt Gail was probably too busy to tell you the rest.'

'Or too discreet,' says my father.

I shrug, but then say, 'I admit that the two things, the marriage clause and the other, seemed entwined with my grief. I was grieved that my mother was dead, and the grief couldn't realise itself properly because of the anger. Or, I should say, offence. Not only offence because she didn't trust me to remain unmarried if I pleased, but the greater offence, by far the greater, was that she let me go away without telling me she was dying, and let me stay away until it was over.'

'Well,' says my father in a hushed voice. 'Well.'

He picks up the little elephant, looks at it, then carefully stands it back in place. The silence grows. I am telling myself ferociously that I will not, cannot, burst into tears. I bend my head and pick at a loose thread on one knee of my jeans.

'You won't have anything,' I hear him ask absently. 'Soda? Fruit juice?'

I shake my head.

'Yes,' he murmurs, 'I think you could call that high-handed. On the face of it, yes.'

He gets up and crosses to a cupboard in the opposite wall. He comes back with a can of tomato juice, and pulls the tab off as he sits down.

'And what explanation have you been given for that?'

'Usually, that she wanted so much for me to have that year of uninterrupted travel. I went with five friends, you see, and it took such a lot of arranging, and if it fell through, the six of us would never have got together again.'

'And you weren't convinced by that?'

'I wanted to be. Sometimes I was.'

'But never for long?'

I look at my father, and consider, as he would say, telling him about the nest of baby birds, and the one that always cheeps loudest, and the compulsion of the raggedy mother always to go back and drop food into that gaping beak. I lower my head and pick at that loose thread again. 'Never for long,' I say.

'And what was your own explanation?'

'Quite often, that she thought I wouldn't be up to it.'

'Oh yes?' he says impartially. He is sipping his juice.

'That she had assessed me, and found me lacking.'

'That occurred to you lately?'

'Yes. Lately.'

'Assessment,' he says, 'is a word in the air at the moment.' He takes another sip of tomato juice. 'My poor child,' he says, 'I suspect you are going to be a writer.'

My mother once made the same proclamation, but did not persist against my disinclination to discuss it. My father persists.

'They do that,' he says. 'They pluck words from the air. They collaborate with accident.'

He is halted by my wide-eyed act, but then says coolly, 'Oh yes, they do. They scavenge. They do. If you don't know it yourself yet, you may take my word for it. The apparent miracle is that when they're in the vein, the scavenged word is so often the right one. But you are wise to avoid discussing it. Very wise. It might be only a phenomenon of youth. It might all come to nothing. Indeed, indeed, it usually does. The poet and novelist, for example, becomes the very minor historian. And in such cases, what appears to be our superstitious and respectful avoidance is shown to have been merely sensible prudence. Yes, yes, you are wise in your avoidance. Now, to backtrack a little, do you have any other evidence for your opinion that Chris was assessing you, and deciding you wouldn't be up to it?'

I hesitate, my mind snaggled on what he has said. He has to repeat the question before I reply.

'Yes. There was a look she used to give me, just before I went away.' In my voice I hear doggedness, almost a sullenness. 'As if she couldn't really see me. As if I had turned into an object.'

For the first time, my father smiles. 'But I remember that look of Chris's,' he says.

He sounds refreshed, slightly amused. 'I remember it well.'

'Uncle Nick says he remembers it, too. But only when he was a child. He says she used to look like that at familiar household objects, and once, he says, at him.'

'And at me, certainly. Now, let us consider. Her young brother, her lover, and her daughter. So perhaps that look was a by-product of intimacy. A useful ability. And for certain people, necessary, as intimates should allow. Yes, indeed. Since we are speaking of entitlements. Did you see that look of hers as one of assessment at the time?'

I almost wish I could say yes. I am reluctant to admit to the sagacity of this man sitting there so vain and neat and jaunty, sipping from a can. So I am silent. He does his one-eyebrow trick again and says, 'Didn't someone tell me you went to a therapist? What did she or he have to say about this?'

But I won't give Mr Parry's theory, in case my father should begin to modify his accordingly. I say, 'He didn't know her, you see.'

'I agree. I agree. Intimates are best. If you will allow them to be honest. Now, if you didn't see that look as an assessment –' The word amuses him. He smiles as he repeats it. 'An assessment at the time, then perhaps, quite lately, you fed the assessment in yourself?' He puts down the empty can and says jovially, 'Eh?'

I return to picking at that loose thread. 'I suppose it is possible,' I say.

'Certainly. Now, myself,' I hear him say, 'I think we should concentrate on that characteristic of Chris's we have called high-handedness. You believe, and I agree, that leaving you in ignorance, and perhaps also that marriage clause, was high-handed. Yet would you say that high-handed actions were common with her?'

'No,' I say. I raise my head. Again we are conspirators. 'No. That's just what's so inexplicable. On the contrary.'

'Quite so. Nor did I find it a common characteristic. On the contrary, as you say. Chris was so courteous, so fair. In my experience, she displayed that high-handedness only once. And that was when she wanted something so much that her need overcame her scruples. Now, let us consider the implications of that.'

He puts up a hand to stop me from speaking. 'It could be,' he says, 'that she employed it so seldom that nobody in her family, even you, had a chance to observe it, let alone to think of it as a characteristic.'

'Yet.' Again he puts up that hand. 'Yet, as you are just about to remark, I had the chance to observe it. Because, as you will also have perceived, she acted in precisely the same high-handed way when she decided to have you. Quite simply and plainly, she used me. Now, it wasn't Chris's habit to use people. Nobody could have been less of a manipulator than Chris. I wish you would have a cup of coffee.'

Almost violently, I cry out, 'I don't want coffee.'

From his chair at the end of the desk, he leans forward and takes my hand from the knee of my jeans. 'There is a great philosophical pleasure,' he says, 'almost an aesthetic pleasure, in contemplating the dominance of the genes.'

I am so impressed that I look sideways at the floor and slide my hand from his as if hoping he won't notice.

'Now I think we must ask ourselves,' I hear him say, 'what Chris wanted so very very much when she kept you in ignorance. She was dying. She knew it. Now, did she want to die alone? What do you think?'

I say, bewildered, that I suppose it is possible.

'Certainly it is possible. It must be assumed, mustn't it? that since people have widely differing characters, they also have widely differing needs. And it is surely reasonable to suppose that not everyone wants his or her family clustered around them at that time. It is surely reasonable to suppose that some may prefer to say their farewells in their own way, and to leave the rest of it, the actual dying business, to trusted professionals. Yes indeed. But sometimes it's the family who won't allow it. They see it as reflecting badly on them.'

My father pauses. Then he says, 'Perhaps you felt something of that reflection yourself. Don't answer if you don't want to.'

Yet he waits before he goes on. 'I'm not implying that Chris was casual about her death. She would be the very person to regard it with respect. Such a mundane yet mysterious event. Yes, Chris would

177

appreciate that. Was anyone there?'

'They all knew. They weren't kept in ignorance. They were on call.'

'But at the actual time?'

'As it happens, no. Her doctor was there. A nurse.'

My father gives a short appreciative laugh. 'It's too bad,' he says, 'that even at a time like that, we should be at the mercy of the expectations of our society.'

I take a deep breath. He raises that eyebrow again and says, 'Tell me, please, Cecily, does what I have said conform, do you think, to your knowledge of Chris's character?'

I take another deep breath. 'What you've said is more plausible than anything anyone else has said. It *would* be like her. I see that. But if it's true, couldn't she have left me a letter? Saying, Sorry, but this is the way I want it? Something like that?'

He looks at me, then clasps his hands on the desk so abruptly that the little elephant falls on its side and sends its pile of papers fanning out. He says, 'Pain?'

'Her doctor says they managed that well.'

My father makes a face and repeats, Managed it well, as if once again saying, Pain. Then he sighs and says, 'You're right about the letter. But perhaps in the intensity of her need, she may simply have failed to consider your feelings, as once, because of a comparable intensity, she failed to consider mine. Did you ever doubt that she loved you?'

I shake my head.

'Never?' he asked.

So I have to say it. 'Never seriously.'

'Why not trust to that then? Remember, we're speaking of entitlements.'

'I want to know the truth.'

'You'll never know the simple verbal truth. Yet you may arrive at an answer. In your search for an answer, have you made any progress?'

'Yes,' I say.

'Even, perhaps, today?'

'Yes,' I say.

'That will keep on. Very often, in these obscure matters, we have all the information we need. But there remains the delicate business of reaching it. And that, unfortunately, doesn't depend on willpower. Don't rush at it. You'll only scatter it. Well, I won't ask again if you want coffee, but I've arrived at the stage where I very definitely do.'

And he gets up, saying, aloof with weariness, 'Excuse me, Cecily.'

But he has taken only a few steps across the room when he turns and confronts me. 'Now,' he says. And he extends an arm, gesturing urgently. 'Now, don't you agree? Don't you? That if Chris could know the offence she has given you? Don't you agree that she would be sorry? And would tell you so?'

He doesn't wait for an answer, but as he turns away he raises that arm above his head, and flicks that hand, his first sign of impatience, or perhaps anger.

And because he has made me see that other extended arm, my mother's and her quick step as she came towards the train, and to hear the warmth and openness of her regret as she spoke, in those forgotten words, her apology for causing my infantile offence, I want, again, to burst into tears. But not in the presence of my father. Having come with the intention of blaming him, and having been brought to a full stop, and then pulled – physically, I feel – pulled and crowded into an area of confusion, and then, mercilessly, out again, I have had all I can bear of my father, and by his last gesture he has made it clear that he has had all he can bear of me. He is opening the cupboard in the opposite wall. Even his back looks angry. I get up and call out, 'Please, where is the lavatory?'

He points without turning. His voice is curt. 'Out that door and first to the right.'

In the lavatory, I sit on the toilet, fluid coming from all directions. My tissues are downstairs in my pack, so I wipe my eyes and blow my nose, in a soft inhibited way, on toilet paper, while saying to myself, Enough. Enough of this.

I am working really hard at controlling this weeping. I don't want to be distracted by responses to my tears. I want to keep intact what I have been shown. I remind myself that even if I get away dry-eyed from my father, I have still to pause in that kitchen doorway, under the scrutiny of strangers, perhaps even blood strangers, and bend to pick up my pack. And I have still to dodge Kirsty's sympathy.

As in the dentist's chair I project onto an image of myself enjoying an evening meal, so now I project onto an image of myself walking composedly and alone up those commonplace, sharp-edged concrete steps, settling the straps of my pack. It is still a warm windy day in my projection, and I see myself reaching the head of the steps and walking out into Foss Street. I walk out of Foss Street and reach the downward slope, and here all I have to do is lean backwards and put one foot forward.

As I raise my face to the sunny air and put that foot forward, my composure returns, and it is not hard to leave the lavatory and open the door of my father's room.

I see him, in profile, still at the cupboard. I call out, 'I think I should go now,' and, encouraged that my voice is steady, I add, 'The exams, you know.'

He turns towards me, a steaming coffee jug in one hand, a cup in the other.

'Of course, the exams. You'll see Kirsty on your way out.'

He sounds relieved. I shut the door on that image of him, and it stays with me as I turn away. There he stands, jug in one hand, cup in the other, and his feet, set apart in their swaddling shoes, as white as wedding cakes.

I am gratified by the simile, its amiable ridicule, and repeat it as I go down the stairs. As white as wedding cakes. Then I walk rapidly, before I can lose my wonderful nerve, along the hall. At the kitchen door I stop and simultaneously reach down to retrieve my pack, my eyes raised and searching for Kirsty.

I have to search because that kitchen is full of people. A television screen high on one wall is giving off its noise and lurid flashes, and Janet Canning is standing to watch, her little kangaroo hands still curled against her chest, and from some kind of raised container in a corner, an infant's leg is waving. Robert and Clare, if still there, are undistinguishable among so many. It is like the scene you sometimes see imprisoned by your eyelids just before you wake up, a crowd of people you have never seen before, but who would be recognisable again. I am goggling, and picking up my pack, when I see Kirsty detach herself from this crowded scene. And then she is standing between me and them, and is saying, 'You want to go now, Cec?'

Then, either of my own volition or hers, we are in the corridor, walking towards the laundry. 'But you'll come again,' she is saying.

'Yes please,' I say. 'After the exams.'

She laughs and says they would all be hard at it in the weekend. As we pass through the narrow larder she puts an arm round my waist, and when we reach the outside door, I believe she is about to kiss me, but after a momentary flare of understanding in her eyes, she refrains. I am grateful for her understanding. A plane passes over the house, and she sets both hands inches from her ears, in token protest, while she shouts, 'No need to ring first. But in case you want to.'

And she takes a card from a breast pocket in her beautiful dress and puts it in the pocket of my shirt.

I smile and lift a hand as I step out of the door. And when I begin to walk up those steep commonplace concrete steps, I actually am able to fuse with that projection of myself, and to walk with composure, settling the straps of my pack.

Though I wonder at the success of it, and slightly suspect a postponement.

I wonder also if I really saw, among those faces in the kitchen, the face I saw last night in the Red Rose and this morning in the laundromat, or if I have, in those few intense moments, somehow imposed his image on the scene.

But when I reach the top and hear footsteps behind me, and I turn and see him coming up fast, in a knees-up run, I am not surprised, and merely note with cautious interest that he has changed from a red to a blue T-shirt.

He starts speaking before he reaches me. 'Say nothing till I've explained. I saw you in the Red Rose last night.'

He has arrived, and stands facing me. 'And in the laundromat this morning. Both times I wanted to speak to you. But what to say? It's pretty hard to just bowl up to someone and say, Hi, I'm your half-brother.'

'It would be,' I say, looking up at him with my stunned or economical attention.

'And say if it turned out I wasn't? Though I was pretty sure last night, as soon as I saw your face. Dad's face. That's got to be her, I said to myself. Cecily Ambruss. But this morning, when my staring drove you out of the laundromat, I thought I had better lay off. My name's David, by the way. David Huth.'

I take his extended hand. 'Hello, David,' I say calmly.

'And,' he says, 'I'm the last-born of Dad's second wife, the one he refers to as the amazingly fecund Marcia. I'm within days of being your twin, did you know that?'

It is, as in my projection, still a warm sunny day. I feel the wind in my hair and the sun on my face as I smile and say, 'No, I didn't know that.'

'Well, I am. I don't live down there with them, by the way. Though I'm staying there till the exams. Quieter. I live near you, in fact. Are you getting the bus?'

'Yes,' I say.

He nods towards the garage. 'Run you down.'

I wait outside the garage, blinking up at the sun, until an old blue car emerges. As I get in, David Huth says, 'Dad won't mind, I don't think. How did you get on with him?'

'All right,' I say, 'considering.'

'He's not so bad. I grew up thinking he was cold and cruel and miserly and all the other things. But then I came up here and got to know him, and realised he's got a point of view. Yeah. At first, though, I was peeved as anything because he didn't include me in the count of his progeny. Am I okay on that side?'

We are coming out of Foss Street. I look out and say, 'Yes, okay. I thought it was me he didn't include.'

'No, definitely me. No question at all about that,' says my loquacious half-brother. 'It irked me considerably. Then I decided to hell with it, and stopped caring. I'll tell you one thing about him. He's intelligent, and that's got to count for something. He says things you remember. Steep bloody hill this.'

'Yes,' I say.

'And I'll tell you another thing about him. He's got a lot to learn about putting material on disc. Such as everything. After the exams, I'm going to give him a hand.'

'I thought Jerome was going to do that,' I say.

'No. Dad doesn't know it yet, but Jerome can't get away.'

And now it occurs to me that I shall certainly know who Jerome is, and who Robert and Clare are, and whose is the infant with the waving leg, as well as the identity of the others in that kitchen. Time will disclose all that. Casually but completely, I put my trust in time. The car is travelling high on the headland, and David Huth is still talking, when I look downwards and see that the surf is flatter now, and that the spume dashing upwards from the rocky projection is less forceful than before. I hear my half-brother saying he is at the University of New South Wales, and at the same time the name of the rocky projection slides into my mind.

'Biology,' says David. 'Still only second year because I took a year off.'

I murmur, 'Me too,' without looking away from those rocks, which of course are known as Wedding Cake Island. I smile to myself at my collaboration with accident.

'Trouble is,' says David 'I'm one of those people who during stu-vac finds all kinds of urgent and extraneous things to do.'

We are descending, and the sea is obscured by land and buildings. 'I'm a bit like that, too,' I say.

'Like your instinct was against it.'

When we come to a stop in Arden Street, he looks worried, and mutters that he doesn't think you're allowed to stop here, so I am ready to say Goodbye, and Thank you, and See you, when he half-turns in his seat, and drapes an arm over the wheel, and says, 'I saw Wil Meade with you last night. You live with him, don't you?'

I nod and wait, my fingers curled upwards in the latch of the door.

'I met him once in Canberra,' says my half-brother, in the respectful tone I am used to. 'Couple of years back. Talking about how the Indonesian settlers, with our complicity, are pushing the West Irian people back from their coast. With our complicity, that's the point. Just like our first settlers did to our Aborigines. He's terrific, Wil Meade. I've always wanted to meet him again.'

'Do you mind if I don't tell him that,' I ask, 'till after the exams?'

The car seems as conscious as I am of its illegal position. It is quivering. But David Huth now seems perfectly at ease. 'God no,' he says, 'Wouldn't expect it.'

'But between the end of the exams and early December, when Wil goes grape-picking, there'll be some free time for sure. We're in the phone book under Ambruss. So, see you then, David.'

As I say his name, I look into his face, and suddenly feel incredulous. He sees my incredulity, and looks shy. 'Terrific, isn't it?' he says. 'What are you doing while Wil's away?'

'A bit of waitressing. But for a long time I've had some papers cluttering up the place, and I'm taking this chance to put them in order.'

He grins and gives a backward nod. 'Like him.'

I laugh and say, 'Nothing so complex. Mine is a matter of simple chronology.'

And I see it as so beautiful, that arch of simple chronology, and so intact, that I hurry on to say, 'Just sort of travel notes. Wil and I share a work table see? and for once I'll have it all to myself.'

He gives his backwards nod again. 'But you'll be visiting up there?'

'Yes. I told Kirsty I would. Only I want to work a few things out first.'

'Naturally,' he says, 'I was like that myself.'

But he is now becoming as uneasy as the car, and is looking nervously about him. So I open the door and get out. Then I stand back, and we each raise a hand to the other as he drives away.

Turning, walking to the bus stand, I see him, now that he is no longer there, with wonderful clarity. I see his arm draped over the wheel, see his inquiring eyes, see his lips move in speech. And I move my own lips to silently pronounce his name: David Huth, envoy from the crowded kitchen, and the most amazing addition to the list of things I shall not yet tell Wil.

The bus is fairly crowded, and I look out of the window pondering on how to provide myself, while Wil is away, with the kind of underlying distraction I need to concentrate. It will be hot, and the windows will be open, but traffic noises are too intermittent for my purpose. A radio in the bathroom turned onto an FM music station is the closest I get to it until, while the bus is travelling through the city, I remember the fan.

We have a pugnacious little fan which stands on the floor and punches out gusts of air at leg-level. Turned to top speed, it needs another outlet for its energy, so it advances upon you in minute jumps, and every now and again you have to get up and absent-mindedly put it back in place.

Yes, I say to myself. Yes, the fan.

Feeling placid and a bit dreamy, I walk down to George Street and get a westie bus to our stop. In peak hour it is always a relief to walk out of the thick stinking traffic of Parramatta Road into our street, where in the late afternoon the shadows of the tristania trees are aslant across the lesser traffic, and people are coming and going in the little shops.

The old Japanese woman is standing in the door of the laundromat, and when she sees me, gravely bows her head in hail and farewell as she turns to go inside. I stop and examine the trunk of the tristania tree. The small section I exposed this morning is already discoloured, and when I peel off another fragment of bark, the fresh trunk no longer seems to resemble human flesh. I remember the infant's leg waving from its receptacle in the corner of that kitchen, and I reflect that human flesh is unique and unmistakable, and that no other substance in the world is comparable to it.

I recognise this as the kind of thing my mother used to say, but although, as I said to Aunt Gail, I don't deny the influence, I accept that comment as mine alone.

On I go, and as I approach our building, and see by the open windows that Wil is home, that suspended list of things I can't tell him feels a bit oppressive. I will indicate it, touch it lightly, by walking in and saying that human flesh is unique and unmistakable. It will be like dropping into his hand that fragment of bark.

But then, to forestall his logic, I think it would be safer to say, 'Externally, human flesh is unique and visually unmistakable.'

But then again, on our steps, it occurs to me that he will reply, 'Cec, humans are not alone in that. All the species have unique and unmistakable covering.'

And while I am casting around for words to dispute this, he will say, 'For example, the crocodile.'

But then, I decide as I open our door, I shall say, 'Ah, but no crocodile has ever said so.'

However (as she would say) Wil is on the phone, and is holding in his free hand the pages of a letter.

'Please get him to the phone, Mum,' he is saying. 'I don't care how. Just put him on.'

Then he waits, handing me the letter and saying, 'Oh God Jesus I'll kill him.'

Ed writes that he is leaving home and coming to

189

Sydney, getting a lift with Buzzy and arriving Sunday. He writes that he means it this time, no shit, but won't bother us because he will bring his sleeping bag and sleep on our floor, and promises to go out whenever we want to study.

Wil groans as he waits, as theatrical as my father. I go and sit in my place at our work table, lowering my pack to the floor. The red cover of Malory is in front of me, and I don't look aside to see, at the bottom of my pile of books, the thin white line of the airmail pads. But I see it anyway, that layer, in my peripheral vision, and am filled with panic. The conception was so easy, so unmistakable, but that thin white line, even half-seen, has broken the lovely arch and scattered the chronology into wild detail.

I put my elbows on the table and hold my head in my hands as I listen to Wil saying fondly:

'Ed, mate. Got your letter, old feller. Now look, Ed.'

And:

'I'm not saying I don't believe you.'

'When did I say you provoked them?'

And yet, I tell myself, it was all there, complete. It was. I felt it. I felt it take shape.

Wil has raised his voice.

'Yes I know you mean it, mate. That's why I'm so bloody alarmed.'

'Because we can't, feller.'

'Right. Can't and won't.'

I lean sideways, take the notebook out of my pack, and put it beside Malory.

'No mate,' Wil is saying, gentle now. 'No Ed old feller. All I'm saying is wait a bit.

And: 'God yes, Ed. You bet.'

While I am saying to myself that it must still be there, and that yes, yes, it only waits to be recaptured.

Wil sounds happier, and is saying in a singing voice, Yeah, yeah, and is telling Ed just to hang on for a bit.

'Just do that, mate.'

'Good old feller. Yeah. Yeah.'

'Great. Great, Ed. That's showing your intelligence. That's the shot.'

'Sure. Be in touch. Bye now old feller. Bye.'

Then Wil puts back the receiver, turns to me, spreads his hands, and says, 'There must be a solution, apart from sending them back to work down the mines. I'll go and shower.'

'Good old feller,' I say. 'Yeah yeah.'

Wil laughs, then gives Malory a nod and says, 'How did you go?'

I say I found nothing I can't fix in the weekend, and this reminds Wil, so that suddenly he is standing tensed, pointing a forefinger at the ceiling, and looking, in his beauty, like a Renaissance angel about to announce.

'I asked them,' I say, 'and they said All over. Finito.'

'Praise God,' says Wil. He comes and sits in his chair, his shoulders forward and his hands loose between his thighs. 'Two whole days of peace and quiet. Am I looking forward to that!'

'Me too,' I say, 'and to the exams.'

'Absolutely. Great to get those behind you.'

I smile and agree. I foresee no end to the things I won't tell Wil, and certainly, this is no time to explain that those two days of hard study, of solving the problem of absorbing one or more instances of magic intervention into my argument, plus the week of exams, had presented themselves to me, as I sat staring at the red cover of Malory and listening to Wil, as a merciful interval. And that's when I knew that I would take refuge under their compulsion, and meekly accept their strictures, while my coming intention ticked secretly on in another place.

Wil and I probably didn't sit there for as long as it now suits me to conceive. He had bought food, too (in case, he said, I had been too busy to shop) and I see us now as sitting there for a long time, peaceful and tired, too lazy to move, each naming what we had bought, then concocting a meal from the named items, while the windows clicked in their loose frames, and the traffic went by outside. And if this image is itself a bit of a concoction, I shan't quibble. Only conception is pure. Yes. So I will make myself get up now, and turn off the fan.

ALSO BY JESSICA ANDERSON

Tirra Lirra by the River   Jessica Anderson

For Nora Porteous, life is a series of escapes. To escape her tightly knit smalltown family, she marries, only to find herself confined again, this time in a stifling Sydney suburb with a selfish, sanctimonious husband. With a courage born of desperation and sustained by a spirited sense of humour, Nora travels to London, and it is there that she becomes the woman she wants to be. Or does she?

The Last Man's Head   Jessica Anderson

Detective Alec Probyn has his enemies. His recent stand on police violence has led to his being suspended from duty but he has a growing suspicion that a vicious crime is about to be committed. How can Probyn prevent this crime and its shattering consequences?

Stories From the Warm Zone and Sydney Stories   Jessica Anderson

Jessica Anderson's evocative stories recreate, through the eyes of a child, the atmosphere of Australia between the wars, and glow with the warmth of memory.

The formless sprawl of Sydney in the 1980s is a very different world. Here the lives of other characters are changed by the uncertainties of divorce, chance meetings and the disintegration and generation of relationships.

Winner of the *Age* Book of the Year Award.

An Ordinary Lunacy   Jessica Anderson

When David Byfield sees Isobel for the first time at a party, he decides that he has fallen in love with her. Months after the party, Isobel's alcoholic husband is found dead in their shabby apartment, an apparent suicide. Then Isobel is accused of his murder and David steps up to defend her both as lawyer and friend. But Isobel's case is more than he bargained for . . .

The Commandant   Jessica Anderson

A story of the penal settlement of Moreton Bay in the 1830s, under the command of fanatical disciplinarian, Patrick Logan. When a young woman with radical ideals joins the community she precipitates the crisis from which the final drama springs.

The Impersonators   Jessica Anderson

Jack Cornock's illness, and his obstinate silence, provoke speculation about his will among the families of his two marriages. Sensitively crafted, *The Impersonators* is a modern novel portraying with humour and perception the fracturing of family relationships and the endurance of love in an increasingly materialistic age.

Taking Shelter   Jessica Anderson

In a novel about and across the generations *Taking Shelter* has our attention from page one.

A group of people, young and old, are drawn together in their quests for permanence, tenderness and love in an era when there are no rules about the age, gender, or the faithfulness of lovers. Written with keen perception, wit and emotional honesty.

It's Raining in Mango   Thea Astley

Cornelius Laffey, an Irish-born journalist, wrests his family from the easy living of nineteenth-century Sydney and takes them to Cooktown in northern Queensland where thousands of diggers are searching for gold in the mud. The cycles of generations turn, one over the other. Full of powerful and independent characters, this is an unforgettable tale of the dark side of Australia's heritage.

Facing the Music   Andrea Goldsmith

'If people do not know your passions they cannot covet them, neither can they spoil them.'

Composer Duncan Bayle has a passion for music. He is admired and famous but his genius has faltered. Juliet Bayle is passionate about Duncan. She shares his success but lives in his shadow. Anna, their talented daughter and once an inspiration to her father, has disappeared.

If Duncan is to create his greatest work Anna must return, but she had good cause to leave and even better reason to stay away.

Facing the Music explores the dark side of ambition and the ambiguous passions that surround creativity. What is a fair price for an artistic life? And who should pay?

Still Murder   Finola Moorhead

A murder story with a difference: a body is found by a nun, a woman is in a mental hospital but is she insane? A psychological thriller using the voices of the victim, confessor, detective, suspects and killer. Confessions and obsessions but is it a murder?

I for Isobel   Amy Witting

A novel about a young girl growing up in Sydney in the 1950s. Each chapter paints a picture of Isobel as she grows to self-awareness and emerges from the false image imposed by her mother.

Marriages   Amy Witting

In this collection of stories Amy Witting deals with the ties that bind, chafe or strangle: marriage and mateship, love and hate, tyranny and charity.

Gracious Living   Andrea Goldsmith

Elizabeth Dadswell, born to the establishment but no longer part of it, is happy – she's divorced and a successful artist.

Adrian, her former husband, is happy: he owns a fantasy holiday resort. Their disabled daughter, Ginnie, is not sure of happiness, but she's only eighteen and in love for the first time. And Kate Marley is happy and shouldn't be – but her disappointments and failures have been annulled by an easy life.

At parties, society weddings and the opening of Adrian's Eden Park Resort, people jostle together in the bourgeois pursuit of happiness.

This is gracious living at its best. Or is it?

Modern Interiors   Andrea Goldsmith

A novel about the dangers and deceits of families, the powerful ties that bind and the emotions that separate. The Finemore family are torn apart when the patriarch, George Finemore, dies suddenly leaving the family to squabble over the estate and his widow, Philippa, decides to broaden her life.